Praise for *Kofi and*

GW00725481

'A cracking bo(
characters ar(
Frank Cottrell-Boyce

'A laugh-a-minute story **not to be missed**.'
The Irish Examiner

'**Fizzing with originality** and energy, this is a perfect
mix of music, friendship and humour.'
Katya Balen

'Perfectly blends **a riotous classroom romp**, a warm
celebration of friendship and a subtle social message.'
The Big Issue

'Joyous, **HILARIOUS** ... it'll inspire a whole generation of
music-lovers, rappers and poets.'
Rashmi Sirdeshpande

'Packed with snappy, witty dialogue that crackles off the page,
and full of humorous scenes, this is **a truly engaging read**.'
BookTrust

'**Hilarious** and full of heart.'
A. M. Dassu

'Entering the **action-packed fun** world of Kofi's family and
friends through this superbly crafted story will be a joy for all.'
The School Librarian

'This is **a must** for all music lovers.'
Just Imagine

For children of the past, and adults of the future.

First published in 2024
by Faber & Faber Limited
The Bindery,
51 Hatton Garden,
London, EC1N 8HN
faber.co.uk

Typeset in Garamond by M Rules
Printed by CPI Group (UK) Ltd, Croydon CR0 4YY

A CIP record for this book is available from the British Library

ISBN 978–0–571–36737–5

MIX
Paper | Supporting
responsible forestry
FSC® C171272

Printed and bound in the UK on FSC® certified paper in line with our continuing
commitment to ethical business practices, sustainability and the environment.
For further information see faber.co.uk/environmental-policy

2 4 6 8 10 9 7 5 3 1

KOFI and the SECRET RADIO STATION

JEFFREY BOAKYE

faber

Summer, 1995

1

Run!

'*Come on!*'

Kofi was wild-eyed with full-blown panic as he skidded round the corner, the weight of the plastic cool box almost pushing him down the sharp concrete steps. His best friend, Kelvin, grimaced with the strain as he tugged hard on the white plastic handle, doing his best to stop the whole thing from toppling over.

The cool box was blue and white and about the size of a small wardrobe on wheels. It was way too big for two twelve-year-old boys to be dragging from one estate to another. But somehow, that was exactly what they were doing.

'The ramp, *the ramp*!'

Kofi glanced over his shoulder, looking past Kelvin at the group of boys gaining pace on them. They were running now, and they meant business. Kofi was thinking fast. If they could get to the ramp, he had an idea . . .

'W-what ram—'

Kelvin's question was cut short as Kofi wrestled the box on to a downwards-sloping ramp and gravity happily took over.

Instinctively, Kelvin shifted his whole body weight on top of the bulky box. Kofi had the exact same idea, and was clinging to the box from the other side. The ramp was steeper than either boy had realised. There wasn't even enough time to scream as the two boys found themselves riding the blue-and-white cool box down through the walkways of an unfamiliar estate.

'KELVIN!' yelped Kofi over the rumble of the plastic wheels. 'Don't let go!'

'I – wasn't – planning – to!' managed Kelvin in response. Not for the first time, he wondered to himself how on earth Kofi had managed to talk him into this.

Behind them, the group of boys were gaining

on them. Kofi hadn't counted how many of them there were, but it looked like a lot, and they weren't stopping. See, this was why you didn't cut through unfamiliar estates, even in the daytime. It made you a target.

'*Corner!*' both boys shouted at once. They hadn't realised the sloping walkway had a right angle at the bottom and there wasn't time to slow down. Without a second thought, Kofi and then Kelvin jumped off and away from the cool box, which continued to roll at top speed. Time stood still as Kofi winced, waiting for the sound of an impact. His eyes were still scrunched shut when he felt Kelvin's sharp elbow jab twice into his side.

'L-look,' Kelvin breathed, pointing at the end of the empty ramp.

The cool box had somehow managed to turn the corner.

'What a clever box,' whispered Kofi in wonder. Then before he could say anything else, the sound of multiple car horns cut through the air.

Kofi and Kelvin briefly looked at each other, open-mouthed. Then they took off at a sprint around the corner. Moments later, the estate boys reached the same spot, gasping for breath, hands on both knees.

'Why they running, man?' the one in front said, breathing deeply. He held up a small silver key to his equally breathless friend. 'They dropped this. I only wanted to give it back.'

2

The Box, the Bus Stop and the Chatty Old Man

For a split second neither boy could see any sign of the cool box, and everything on the high street looked as normal as ever. Which was weird because they had just sent a three-foot-high plastic tub on wheels straight into oncoming traffic.

Then Kelvin spotted it. It had come to rest next to a bus stop. An old man with a red silk scarf was sitting beside it, on the bench. He was pale and frail, with battered leather shoes and a worn-out old jacket. It was a funny image: the man and the cool box looked like old friends. Kofi jogged over, with Kelvin not far behind.

'This yours?' the old man croaked through a lipless smile, thumbing towards the box. He had more gums than teeth. Kofi inspected the box for damage, noticing that the grey old man's bright red scarf was the only pop of colour on him.

'Um, yeah,' said Kofi absently.

'Picnic?' the man asked Kelvin.

Kelvin breathed twice before answering.

'Something like that.'

The old man looked the cool box up and down, taking in its size, then at the two boys, then back to the trolley again. Kelvin gave a flat smile.

'We're really hungry,' he said.

A bus pulled up and the old man rose unsteadily to his feet to get on. As the bus pulled away, the boys hoisted the box on to the smoothest part of the pavement and set about continuing their journey, trundling along.

'That was cool,' said Kofi once they had got moving properly.

'What? P-pushing the box into a bus stop?'

'No,' laughed Kofi. 'The way you talked to that old man.'

Kelvin looked at his shoes, embarrassed. Kofi had been helping him with his stutter all summer long. Kofi was the only person Kelvin knew who seemed to see past it, and he'd made it something like a mission to help him get over it. It was one of the reasons they were such good friends. For all the bad ideas and mad schemes, Kofi really was the best friend Kelvin had ever had.

'I know,' mumbled Kelvin, feeling a flush that had nothing to do with the sun. 'Thanks.'

Kofi smiled. 'Right, then,' he said with a quick rub of his palms. 'We need to get going before everyone leaves.' He patted the cool box and squinted up briefly towards the bright midday sun. 'Let's go.'

3

A Gap in the Market

On what was definitely now the hottest day of the year, it wasn't only the mid-afternoon sun that was making the boys sweat. After the rampway escape, the cool box now had a wheel that was twisted slightly to one side, meaning they had to drag it rather than roll it across the broken paving slabs and uneven concrete. Every half turn, it would make a little squeak as though it was in pain. The boys knew how it felt.

It had been an impossible task since they had first left their estate, but this close to their destination, and after all that drama, it felt silly to give up now. Whenever Kofi got an idea in his head, he'd always see it through. And whenever Kelvin promised to help with something, he never let you down.

Kofi put up a hand for moment, letting his head drop forward, signalling to stop.

'Almost there,' he gasped, running a damp forearm across his brow. 'Promise.'

Kelvin looked at him through half a squint.

'Y-you wish,' he replied sarcastically. He gave the trolley a tug and the twisted wheel squeaked back in agreement.

'Don't you start,' muttered Kofi to the cool box. 'Come on.'

It was Sunday afternoon and they were on their way to the pitches – a collection of mini concrete football pitches and basketball courts that had been set up by the council over the summer. It wasn't much, but local kids from all the surrounding estates had flocked there since it opened. Every weekend, you'd get groups of kids milling around, playing or eating snacks, or just chatting. Then there were the baller boys who would turn up in full sportswear to play serious games of football or basketball, and everyone would watch, like an audience. When they were playing, little kids like Kofi and Kelvin weren't allowed on – that was the unspoken rule. But it was still cool just to hang out and soak up the atmosphere.

Today, Kofi was working. His face lit up as they rounded the corner away from the high street towards the park.

Customers, he thought greedily, his eyes scanning the scene. The pitches were packed with kids of all ages, no adults at all. A big game of basketball was in full flow on the main court and crowds of boys and girls were watching on. Smaller games were taking place on the other pitches and courts, and some groups were sitting scattered on nearby patches of grass. It was a perfect summer scene, and Kofi had pound signs in his eyes.

'Let's go stand over there,' he said, pointing at a tree to one side of the main court.

The two boys made the final drag over to Kofi's chosen spot and let the cool box fall against the tree with a last squeak. Kofi was animated now. He shrugged his backpack off his shoulders and unzipped it hastily.

Naturally more cautious, Kelvin looked around, subconsciously scanning for danger. He never would have done this kind of thing alone, but with Kofi, he let himself get carried away. It had happened last year – first with the arcade tournaments, and then the

Paper Jam magazine. Kofi always had some scheme he was cooking up. And to be fair, they usually ended up making good money.

Kofi was busy unpacking his bag. He was excited.

'OK, so let's tie the sign up there. We'll use one of your shoelaces.'

He carefully unrolled a big piece of paper that had been written on with bright felt tips. ICE POLES, it said in huge, colourful letters. 15p EACH. Kofi had made them at home the night before, filling the freezer with blocks of fruit-flavoured water.

Kofi looked up at Kelvin with a twinkling eye and dark smile, producing a thick black marker from a side pocket.

'We'll cross out the 15p and make it 10p,' he said. 'That way people will think it's a bargain and buy more.'

Kelvin suddenly spotted something.

'K-Kofi . . .' he started. Kofi didn't stop.

'. . . and then later we can bring it down to 5p when everyone's tired. I've even got the 5p's ready for change.'

'Kofi—' Kelvin tried again. Kofi was oblivious.

'*Kofi Mensah* . . .' he said to himself happily. 'The biggest business genius on the block . . .'

Kelvin tugged at his sleeve. Kofi didn't even notice, wrapped up in his latest enterprise.

'... Actually, we might need to make sure we don't use up all the change to begin with. Come to think of it, we—'

'KOFI!'

This time the voice wasn't Kelvin's. Kofi spun around to be confronted with a sight he hadn't expected to see. It was his sister, Gloria, accompanied by her best friend, Shanice. Shanice was a proper rudegirl. She fixed him with a stare that could have melted every single ice pole.

'What are *you* doing here?'

The siblings spoke at the same time, and Kelvin suddenly realised how similar they were. At fourteen years of age, Gloria was technically Kofi's big sister, but he was now a fraction taller than her. Which Kofi loved reminding her of.

'You told Dad you were sick. That's why you couldn't go to church.'

The statement was an accusation. Gloria stood with her arms folded, resting her weight on one hip. In that moment, she looked scarily like Mum.

Kofi looked to Kelvin in a mild panic. His friend shrugged. 'Start coughing?' he whispered.

Kofi began scrabbling around for an excuse, beads of sweat breaking out across his forehead.

'Um, I, I – I was sick, this morning I mean, but then I, um . . .'

He noticed her notice the cool box.

'Is that Mum's good icebox?'

Her eyes widened.

'Is that *my* black pen?'

Kofi put both hands up and then clasped them together. He knew *I'm telling Mum* was coming next. Then he remembered something.

'Wait, aren't you supposed to be at her place doing homework?'

He pointed at Shanice, who batted his finger away.

'*Her*, you know,' she said with a look like a bad smell had just entered her nostrils. 'I beg you don't get rude.'

Now it was Gloria's turn to panic.

'I – I – I was, but then . . . anyway, what are you doing here? You selling ice poles?'

'Wow, you're clever,' Kofi said sarcastically, receiving a clap to the back of the head for his troubles.

Kelvin stepped in while Kofi pouted and rubbed his neck with his spare hand. Kelvin had long ago learned that when you got to this point, honesty was always the best policy.

'Yes, we're selling ice poles,' said Kelvin, responding to Gloria's question. 'It was Kofi's idea. Every time w-w-we come to the pitches people get th-thirsty but the – the nearest shop is ages away.'

Kofi shrugged. 'Gap in the market,' he concluded. 'See?'

He pointed at the sign and leaned forward to open up the box. Then he realised. No key.

He patted his pockets, looking to Kelvin for help.

Gloria sighed. 'Here.'

Gloria carefully removed a hairpin from the back of her head and stooped down to ease it into the cheap plastic lock on the cooler's lid. After a few moments it sprang open, and Kofi couldn't help but marvel at how good his sister was at being bad, when she needed to be.

All four faces leaned in and a waft of cool air hit them like a welcome breeze. Bags of colourful ice were tied up and neatly arranged in rows, ready to be sold. Shanice broke the silence.

'You know, your brother's an idiot, Gloria, but truesay he's a clever idiot.'

'Thanks!' Kofi grinned.

'Gimme a red one then,' said Shanice. 'It's bare hot, innit.'

'Shanice!' Gloria protested.

'What?' said the teenager, flicking a hooped earring

out of the way and reaching for an ice pole. 'It's a good idea, innit.'

Kofi pointed to the sign with one hand and put out a palm with the other, indicating payment. Shanice laughed.

'This one's on the house, darling.' She blew him a kiss that he avoided like it was physically airborne. 'Come we go, Gloria.'

As the girls left, Gloria quickly grabbed an orange ice pole and turned with a look that any sibling would know translated as *I won't tell if you don't*. Kofi grimaced back in reluctant agreement. Having an older sister was *tough*.

4

Lyrics for Lyrics

It wasn't long until Kofi and Kelvin were down to their last few poles. It being such a hot, hot day, everyone at the pitches was glad to be able to quench their thirst without making the trek to the nearest corner shop, even if it meant paying 10p. Kofi had been his usual energetic, charming self and had sold the goods easily. He had his one-liners down pat, and was enjoying playing the salesman.

'*I – C – E, only 10p!*'

Or:

'You look cool enough already, but you know what'd you make you even cooler?'

Or even a little remix he made up for the occasion: *'Ice, ice baby – only 10p! I've got some ice, ice, baby.'*

Now he had the money stowed away in the secret lining of his rucksack. He'd carefully stuffed it with toilet paper the night before to make sure you couldn't hear the coins jangle. He was a little kid on the ends. You couldn't be too careful out here.

Soon enough, Kofi and Kelvin were sitting on their haunches under the shade of the big tree. Most of the matches had finished but there were still lots of kids milling about. Kofi was happy doing one of his favourite things: spotting trainers he liked and talking about which ones he wished he had. Kelvin wasn't that interested in trainers at all, but he enjoyed keeping Kofi company.

A sudden *oooooh* from a nearby crowd interrupted Kofi's chatter. Both boys looked up. They recognised the scene at once.

'Is that . . . a cypher?'

Kofi strained to have a closer look. Cyphers had become a big thing at his school last year, after Kelvin had introduced rapping into the playground cussing-match battles. Now it looked like everyone was doing them in the parks and estates – meeting up to rap together in a friendly competition of flows.

'I don't think so . . .' replied Kelvin, suddenly alert. 'It looks more like . . . a *clash* . . . Lemme go see . . .'

'No – Kelvin, wait!'

But it was too late. Kelvin had already risen to his feet, drawn as though to a magnet to the rappers on court one. Clashes were very different to cyphers. Clashes were full-blown lyrical warfare, with insults and disses traded with wit and venom. Kelvin was a natural wordsmith and loved the aggression of battle rap, even though he was such a quiet person. But Kofi knew that clashes could get dangerous. Especially with people you didn't know. Kofi did a quick sign of the cross and looked up at the skies with his palms pressed together.

'Please don't let us get beaten up,' he mumbled, before scrambling to his feet and jogging after his friend.

The crowd was split into two roughly equal groups, standing opposite each other in half-open semicircles. In the middle were two boys, facing off. Kofi recognised one of them from Year 11 at his school, St Campions. He was lanky with a sloping high-top. His opponent was short and stocky, clutching a basketball that he passed from hand to hand while he rapped. The audience were pulsing to a beat being drummed out on hands and feet. The atmosphere was electric but tense. The clash was in full flow.

'Look at you, thinking you could
ever come and rap at me
Why are you so lanky, man – your
head is gonna smack a tree
My rhymes are so expensive but you
know I'm gonna clash for free
And everybody here is definitely
gonna clap for me . . .'

The stocky baller was giving it his best shot, but he was struggling to get that all-important crowd reaction that you needed to win a clash. High-top didn't hesitate:

'Lanky? What's your problem, man?
Why you sounding so hurt?
Trying to be a baller when you
really need a growth spurt!
My flow's so strong when I rap
it makes my throat hurt
You're gonna finish last so it makes
sense that I should go first
Little bean-head – you look like a muppet

Everybody laughing when I
rap because they love it.
And everybody's laughing at YOU –
because you're rubbish,
So stop it: and if you can then
try to rise above THIS!'

At this point, high-top produced a twig like a measuring stick and held it above stocky's head. The crowd fell to pieces, holding their hands over their mouths, falling backwards and saying things like *'Ooooh', 'No way'* and *'That was cold'*. It was a decisive win. The stocky baller was looking around helplessly, realising the extent of his defeat. At this point, Kofi was doubled over in fits of laughter at the twig punchline, nudging Kelvin with his elbow.

The stocky baller fixed his attentions straight at Kofi. He focused all of his hurt and frustration at this little kid who was daring to laugh at him.

'What you laughing at?'

It wasn't a question. The atmosphere instantly tensed up and Kofi snapped back to reality. The sound of a few people sucking in air could be heard.

'I said, what are you laughing at, *bruv*?'

At the word 'bruv' he flung the basketball in his

hands full force towards Kofi's chest. Kofi had no time to prepare himself – the ball was coming straight at him.

Kelvin's catch was like a clap of thunder. He looked the baller dead in the eye in a way that seemed to say, without words, that he was ready to take up the challenge. The baller blinked twice and everyone stopped. Even Kofi didn't quite know what was going to happen next. The defeated rapper couldn't back down now.

'What, you wanna go? You wanna *clash*?'

The baller started laughing dryly. There was no way this little kid was going to challenge him. This would be easy.

Kofi snatched a glance at Kelvin's face. It was stony and serious, the eyes not blinking, the mouth tight-lipped and ready. He knew what Kelvin was capable of. He was the best rapper at St Campions, when he felt like it. And when he got angry, he could be devastating. Like what happened against Leroy last term, when Kelvin ended up getting punched in the face. If he went for it now, they would *both* definitely get beaten up, Kofi was certain of it.

Kelvin's mouth twitched.

Kofi blinked.

'*Yo.*'

All eyes turned in the direction of the deep, bassy voice that had just interrupted the scene.

Kofi's mouth fell open.

'Leroy?'

5

Leroy's Return

'What are you doing here?'

The boy walking towards Kofi and Kelvin was slightly taller than they were, even though he was the same age. His face was round, as always, but he'd thinned out in the body and had a bit of a teenage swagger about him. He was flanked by a few of the boys who had chased Kofi through the estate, but thankfully, Kofi noticed, they didn't seem to be worried about catching him now.

As Leroy walked, he touched fists with a few boys in the crowd, who clearly knew who he was. Kofi noticed he was wearing a flashy pair of Nike trainers, the ones they called '180s', supposedly because of their price tag. Leroy walked with a confident bop. He approached Kelvin with a half-smile that was directed at the stocky rapper opposite.

'You don't want to mess with this yute, trust me,' he said, taking the ball out of Kelvin's hands and returning it to its owner.

Kelvin was as shocked as Kofi. They hadn't seen Leroy since last year at school, and that was after the famous rap battle that led to Leroy getting suspended.

'Here,' said Leroy, producing a tiny silver key. 'You dropped this.'

'Uh, thanks,' said Kofi, looking from Leroy to the estate boys and back to the key. Leroy continued.

'Seriously, Damon,' he began, addressing the stocky rapper by name. '*The Reloader* is no joke.' He thumbed in Kelvin's direction. 'He's the best rapper in the whole of St Campions.'

'I – I am?'

Kelvin was taken aback. Leroy wasn't known for handing out compliments.

'Blatantly,' said Leroy. Then he launched into a mid-tempo flow that took everyone by surprise:

'Shut your mouth, you know the crowd thinks
That the things that you say
really make the air stink,
My mind's so quick it'll make your eyes blink,
And you smell so bad that we
think you need Lynx.
I can't speak but believe it I can rap it,
I take the biscuit while you're
eating the whole packet,
You try to act tough but you're just a thick dunce,
You skip PE cos you never skip lunch,
I know you can't count so you better skip maths,
But count on this, you could never diss back,
They know it's all facts and I'm
hearing them cheer back
But you still can't hear cos you're
thicker than earwax . . .'

Kelvin's eyes widened in astonishment. It was the *exact* same rap he had levelled at Leroy last year.

'You remembered it?' exclaimed Kelvin.

'How could I forget it?' laughed Leroy. 'Anyway, you're not the only one with a memory, rudeboy.'

Damon and the other rappers were clearly impressed.

'Those really your raps?' asked Damon, his voice softening.

'Yeah,' replied Kelvin and Kofi in unison. Kofi was used to speaking on behalf of his usually quiet friend. He could be a bit like a manager sometimes.

'He comes up with new stuff all the time. I taught him.'

Kelvin looked at Kofi sideways.

'Sort of,' added Kofi.

Damon squinted briefly before speaking with a nod.

'I rate it,' he said finally, offering out a fist for the boys to touch. The tall high-top did the same and soon, everyone was mingling happily, welcoming Kelvin and Kofi into the group.

'Come on,' said Leroy as the crowd started to melt away. 'I'll help you get that box back. It's bigger than Kelvin.'

6

New Friends, Old Friends

It was far easier to get the cool box back to the estate with three people helping, not to mention the fact that it was now completely empty. As they walked, Leroy explained how he had moved into his new estate earlier that year, meaning that he now lived even closer to Kelvin and Kofi. He was also much closer to St Campions, and would therefore more of a familiar face among local kids. Leroy had always been a sociable person, so it was no surprise that he was already making friends with boys from the estate.

Compared to the snarling bully that he had started to become last year, Leroy was like a different person. But even still, Kofi struggled to fully relax and joke around with him.

'Honestly, bro,' smiled Leroy as they manoeuvred the cool box through the walkways. 'When you said I skip PE cos I never skip lunch, I was *dying*. I gave up snacks that same day, bruv.'

'. . . You're . . . welcome?' joked Kelvin, unsure of what to make of the new Leroy.

Leroy made as if to punch Kelvin, making him flinch, before pushing him lightly in the shoulder. Kofi watched on intently, trying to figure it all out. Yes, Leroy seemed to have turned a new leaf, and maybe he had changed his ways, but deep down, Kofi was still uncertain. Leroy had been so cruel to Kelvin at school and even worse that night Leroy and his friends had started trouble with Kofi on the street – when Uncle Delroy had intervened and ended up getting arrested. It was hard to think that Leroy could suddenly be a different person. Not just like that. So no, Kofi didn't trust it. Not yet.

Soon, they got to Leroy's block and said their see-you-laters with a touch of fists, before Leroy disappeared into a waiting group of friends. Kofi and Kelvin hurried on.

'You all right?' asked Kofi over the squeak of the wonky cool-box wheel. 'With Leroy, I mean. He punched you last year, man.'

Kelvin paused before making his reply.

'I think so,' he said cautiously. 'He seems ... OK, but, he, h-he's still Leroy, right?'

'Exactly,' said Kofi, looking behind him. 'Anyway, if he tries anything you should hit him – with some new bars,' he added with a smile. 'I know you have some.'

It was Kelvin's turn to smile.

'I might do,' he grinned.

By the time they got to Kelvin's block, the late afternoon sun was warm and golden, the estate looking almost pretty through all the graffiti and concrete. In the near distance Kofi could make out the hunched figure of Mrs Weaver shuffling their block. Mum always stopped to talk to her on the way back from shopping on a Saturday. As usual, the faint bass of the pirate radio station told Kofi that he was almost home.

'Thanks for today, Kels,' he said, opening his rucksack to give Kelvin's share of the profits to him. 'I'll see you at school.'

And with that, Kelvin was gone, leaving Kofi alone with the empty cool box, the pirate radio bass, and his thoughts.

7

Dad's Big Surprise

'I thought you were sick?'

Kofi wasn't expecting his big brother, Emmanuel, to be home so early. At eighteen years old, Emmanuel was pretty much a third adult in the house, and he was off to university next year. He was supposed to be at church, helping Dad with setting up chairs and stuff. Instinctively, Kofi felt his mind go into overdrive thinking up excuses as to why he wasn't in bed, before he decided that he didn't actually need to make anything up. It was only Emmanuel, after all.

'I *was*,' he replied cheerfully. 'But then I saw Gloria's school picture and vomited my guts out, so I felt better.'

He ducked to avoid the cushion thrown at him by his sister. Gloria was on the sofa in the front room, curled up watching the telly. He scowled at her with a face that said: *You tried to get me in trouble*, and she scowled back with a face that said: *Good*.

The sound of the buzzer interrupted the battle about to happen and all three siblings looked at each other.

'Dad,' they said together.

'Don't let him in yet!' yelped Kofi as Emmanuel rose to go to the door. Kofi was in panic mode, realising he had to make himself look sick to convince Dad of his little lie. He kicked off his trainers and ran into the bedroom he shared with Emmanuel, emerging seconds later with a vest on his body and a pair of pyjama trousers on his legs. His siblings stood there watching him, Emmanuel confused and Gloria shaking her head slowly. Unfazed, Kofi ran into the kitchen and yanked open the fridge freezer, grabbing a carton of orange juice and a bag of frozen mixed vegetables. Emmanuel sighed and went to buzz open the door. The flat was five flights up, so there was time ahead of Dad's arrival.

Before Gloria had a chance to stop him, Kofi had

tipped the bag of veg directly into the kitchen sink, followed by a generous splash of the orange juice.

'Kofi!' his siblings exclaimed.

The front door rattled open and Kofi leaned forward theatrically, clutching his belly in front of the fake vomit.

'Oh, my ... gastric passages ...' he moaned loudly, reaching for the nearest biology lesson he could remember.

At that moment, Dad flew into the flat, clutching a large cardboard box in both hands. He swept past the kitchen excitedly, placing the box on the glass coffee table in the middle of the front room.

'I've bought something,' he said, grinning.

Intrigued, Kofi rose to his feet to join his brother and sister. Dad never came home with new surprises, and he never *ever* spent money that he didn't need to. So this was a big deal.

Three faces peered down at Dad's box as he carefully opened it up, crinkling through sheets of fresh tissue paper.

'There!' he said with unfiltered enthusiasm. 'Our new *camcorder*.'

Kofi gasped with shock. He'd only ever seen one of these on TV. A portable video recorder with little cassette tapes that you slid into the side. It looked expensive. Dad was very excited.

'I offered to help with some events at church and they said they needed a new cameraman,' he explained as he lifted the device out of its polystyrene shell. 'I thought I could do it. And the electrical shop on the high street was open. I'm coming round to shops being open on Sundays now.'

'Cool ...' said Kofi, reaching to push the nearest random button. Gloria smacked his hand out of the way as she retrieved the instructions, which Kofi instinctively snatched out of the box and held out of her reach.

'Whatever you do,' he said seriously, 'don't point it at Gloria. You'll crack the lens.'

'*You two*,' warned Emmanuel, doing his best impression of Mum. Dad was too busy fiddling with his new toy to pay any attention to the squabbling.

In less than half an hour, the Mensah family (minus Mum) had filmed their first set of family videos. A lot of it was just strange camera angles and Dad asking if the camcorder was filming yet, but eventually they had a few good clips of Kofi playing to the camera and making everyone laugh. He was a natural performer and had everyone in stitches with his ridiculous impressions – of family, friends and famous people off the telly. The way he shouted 'Awooga!' like the presenter from *Gladiators* was too funny to handle.

When the door clattered open to signal Mum's arrival back home after work, even Dad was caught off guard. She was a naturally relaxed person, but she definitely liked coming back to a tidy flat after a long shift.

'What's this,' she said, surveying the scene in front of her with a faint smile. Then she drifted into the kitchen and clocked the fake vomit in the sink. Her tone hardened.

'And what is THIS?'

Years of experience told Emmanuel and Gloria what to do. They pointed straight at Kofi.

'*He* did it.'

Mum looked straight at Dad and cocked her head to one side, one hand on her hip. Dad suddenly looked like a naughty schoolboy.

'Yeah, he probably did,' said Dad, nodding.

'*Dad!*' said Kofi.

8

Mr Redge vs Rap Club

Kofi sat uncomfortably on the hard plastic chair. He was tugging at his shirt collar and squirming. The first school assembly of the year was somehow even more boring than he thought it would be, and the collar he'd been told to do all the way up was only making things worse. The whole school was crammed into the hall. Even though it was only the first week of September, it was raining heavily and depressingly grey outside. Kofi sighed. Summer was definitely over.

The head teacher, Mr Redge, was busy saying

something or other with his usual sweaty, permanently annoyed face. He spoke through tight lips as though his back teeth were clenched, and had an expression on his face as if having to talk to his students was getting in the way of his busy day. Kofi noticed that he was fatter and balder than last year, but still just as vicious as ever. Maybe more.

It was only the start of the day, but Kofi was fully ready to go home. He looked around the hall at the bored, blank faces and wondered how on earth he could get through another four years of this. Just as he was about to start counting how many ceiling tiles there were, the word *rapping* snapped him to attention. He listened in to what Redge was actually saying.

'. . . to repeat: *rapping*, or any kind of *battling*, in any of our playgrounds, is *banned*, from today. Banned!'

A low murmur started to ripple through the students, met by teachers turning to say *shh* and making patting-down motions with their hands.

'Quiet!' hissed Redge with a snarl. 'I haven't finished.'

Kofi felt his heart sink. The cyphers and rap battles were the best part of coming to school. He'd already started thinking about starting up a special new edition of *Paper Jam* this year and getting Kelvin to write out all the original lyrics that would be showcased throughout the year. If rapping wasn't allowed, life at St Campions wouldn't be worth living.

A thin arm shot up from somewhere near the front.

'What?' snapped Redge, not even trying to disguise his irritation.

It was Ibby, a student in Year 9 who had started coming to the cyphers near the end of last term. He wasn't cool, but he was a gifted rapper and had even won the respect of the older kids in the years above. That was how it worked.

'Uh, sir, Mr Redge, sir,' he started. A few snickets of laughter rippled through the seats. Ibby continued with a sniff. 'What about Rap Club?'

Ibby pointed a finger at Mr Downfield, Kofi's English teacher, who ran a weekly Rap Club for kids in Years 7, 8 and 9. Like most of the other teachers at school, Mr Downfield was white, but unlike the others he actually took an interest in rap. Everyone's head swivelled in his direction and he instantly blushed a deep red. Mr Downfield used to be Kofi's worst teacher by far, but since he started Rap Club, he hadn't been so bad. It looked like Mr Redge didn't know anything about the club at all.

'What *Rap Club*?' spat Redge.

Kofi groaned.

*

That lunchtime, true to his word, Redge made absolutely sure that no rapping of any description could take place at St Campions that day, or any other. The teachers were out on patrol behind the refectory and whenever they thought anything might happen they would swoop in and shoo the students apart like pigeons.

'I'm starting to think it'd be better to just get suspended,' said Kofi to Kelvin, watching a group of kids kicking a pebble around.

'Don't worry,' Kelvin replied. 'You probably will anyway.'

The next few days were dull and depressing in the life and times of Kofi Mensah. The return to school and end of holidays meant that nothing interesting was happening at all. And now that it was September, he wasn't even able to hang out much at T's house to play *Street Fighter II* on the Super Nintendo. Besides, T still liked to hang around on the estate, which was a definite no-no for Kofi's parents.

Then one day, something happened.

It was Thursday break time. A group of three Year 11s appeared from seemingly out of nowhere and sidled up to Kofi and Kelvin on the sly. One of them was Marlon Richards, the unofficial host of the St Campions cyphers. His usual animated self was quiet as he whispered out of the side of his mouth to Kofi and Kelvin. His voice was gravelly and low, as though every word might get him arrested and thrown into a dusty cell.

'Yo. Car park. Behind the minicab office. High street. After school. Four thirty. Yeah?'

Kofi and Kelvin nodded. They had no idea what they were being invited to, or why.

'And tell that Leroy kid in your year to come too, yeah? He's cool. But no one else.'

Another nod.

Then Marlon and his friends disappeared before a circling teacher could move them on.

Kofi swivelled to face Kelvin. 'Did that just happen?' he said. 'Do we tell Leroy?'

'Tell me what?'

Leroy had appeared between them suddenly, his big arms thrown around both their shoulders from behind. He was breathing heavily, having come straight from playing football with a tennis ball. He was in with the football crowd and, despite everything last year, was still one of the most popular kids in the year. Kofi spoke first.

'Marlon in Year Eleven wants us to come somewhere after school. And he said you should come too.'

Kofi wasn't entirely sure if he wanted Leroy to be there, but as usual he'd spoken without thinking. He couldn't backtrack now.

'You coming?'

Leroy grinned and threw his weight into Kelvin with a full-body shove. 'It's calm,' he said casually, meaning that everything was OK. 'I'm there, man.'

There was an awkward pause.

'Look, man,' said Leroy. 'I wasn't cool with you lot last year. I get it. But we had fun with those arcades, remember?'

Kofi couldn't deny that the tournaments had been a big highlight. Even Kelvin nodded. It really had been fun – until it wasn't.

'I'm different now, innit,' continued Leroy. Then he sighed. 'Sorry I punched you, man.'

He looked at the ground. Kofi made eye contact with Kelvin.

'S'all right, man,' he said. 'Isn't that right, Kelvin?'

Leroy looked up, looking genuinely hopeful. Kelvin opened his mouth to speak. Then he chewed his lip, before carrying on. 'Yeah – OK. S'all right.'

Leroy looked physically relieved and his face brightened.

'Wicked!' he beamed as the bell rang, signalling the end of break. 'All right, come we go.'

Kelvin shot Kofi a worried look. He really wasn't sure about Leroy yet and could sense that Kofi wasn't fully convinced either.

Leroy had already skipped ahead to have one final kick of a playground tennis ball, leaving Kofi and Kelvin.

'I know,' said Kofi. 'You've got a bad feeling about this...'

Kelvin nodded.

'But it could be fun!' beamed Kofi. Kelvin exhaled slowly.

'Trust me?' said Kofi.

And with that, they joined the shuffle back inside for period five.

9

A Car Park Adventure

It had almost caused Kofi physical pain to avoid getting into trouble during period five history, but the effort was well worth it to avoid detention, now that there was somewhere exciting to go after school.

With a head churning full of thoughts, Kofi fell through the school gates and ripped his tie off triumphantly as soon as the teachers were out of sight. As usual, it seemed like most of the school was heading for the newsagent's on the high street to get their fill of sweets, crisps and fizzy drinks. The shopkeeper only let in two at a time, but it didn't stop everyone from flocking to the shop anyway.

Kofi found Kelvin in the bustle and whipped twice at Kelvin's legs with his tie, before Kelvin caught it and yanked it away, handing it back to Kofi. Kofi laughed. He was in a good mood.

'It's got to be something to do with the cyphers,' said Kofi excitedly. 'I think we were the only Year Sevens who got involved with the olders last year.'

'And the Cussing Matches,' added Kelvin.

Kofi thought for a moment, remembering *Cuss Bombs*, the illegal magazine that everyone had loved, which had gotten him into so much trouble last year.

'Hey, maybe the Year Elevens want us to do another magazine,' he thought out loud. 'Is your magic memory still working?'

'You make it sound like I'm a computer,' answered Kelvin.

'You are like a computer,' replied Kofi. 'Come on,' he said, stuffing his tie into his blazer pocket.

They reached the shop and joined a messy queue being policed by Clapman. That's what they called the younger shopkeeper who stood out front like a bouncer. He made sure only two kids went in at a time and clapped them away when they started gathering in large groups. It was busy.

Kids were asking other kids to get them something when they went in, while loud conversations about football, TV and computer games raged on in the background.

Leroy emerged from the shop's entrance, bopping with his casual swagger. He had a big bottle of cola in one hand, ready to swig it. He found himself directly in front of Kelvin. The St Campions' Year 8s didn't need much prompting:

'*Oooh*,' said someone theatrically. 'Rematch!'

'Leroy vs Kelvin!'

'Remember last year!'

'Man got punched!'

'Go on, Leroy.'

'Go on.'

Kofi looked at Leroy. For a split second, he thought he saw the old flash of cruelty, the ready sting of attack. Leroy loved to play to a crowd, and the crowd were waiting, hungrily, for conflict.

But as quickly as he saw it, it was gone. Leroy's face relaxed, breaking into a smile.

'Nah,' he said jovially. 'Me and Kels is cool.'

Kelvin's face was hard to read, but Kofi knew what he was capable of, lyrically, if he was pushed. He stepped forward with both hands clasped together, ready to be the peacemaker.

'Let's go, man,' he said hastily.

This new friendship was going to be a tricky one to manage, he thought to himself.

*

The car park was tucked away deep behind the high street and you had to cut through a series of alleyways to access it. It was hard to find, so it took a short while for the three boys to get there. Kofi would normally have been a bit worried about going to such a deserted location to meet older kids for a mystery reason, but today his curiosity was bigger than his caution. Besides, he had company, which always made things a bit less scary.

They turned a corner into a concrete patch and Kofi gasped. The scene before him was not what he had expected.

There must have been fifty, maybe sixty kids standing around in various sized groups, all in different uniforms from different schools. Judging from their heights, pretty much all of them were from Year 11, with a few Year 10s scattered through. It wasn't just boys either. Kofi could see quite a few girls in the mix, including some from St Ursula's, his sister's school. There was a buzz in the air, a lot like at the pitches during the summer, but here, there were no games to be played.

Marlon Richards was in his element. He was dead centre in the middle of the action, orchestrating events, limbs flailing like an overexcited squid. When Kofi looked carefully, he could see a number of kids who were standing in a loose circle around him, the ones who weren't just watching.

'Whoa,' said Kofi and Leroy at the same time.

'I know,' said Kelvin in agreement, stepping forward like a moth drawn to light. It was the biggest cypher any of them had ever seen. And it was already under way.

The quality was high. By now, Kofi was used to listening to hip-hop and knew a good flow when he heard one. These kids were well practised, each sticking to sixteen bars perfectly and jumping in with skippy flows and cleverly woven punchlines. A dim light from a nearby street lamp offered an atmospheric glow over the scene as the autumn afternoon darkened into grey. Faces were contorted in concentration, controlled aggression and competition. It was electric.

'Ah yes, yes, yes!' chirped Marlon after the round was over, clocking the new arrivals. 'Here come the youngers I was telling you lot about. St Campions don't play! Let's see what you got, rudeboy!'

Kofi froze as he suddenly realised that all eyes were on him, Kelvin and Leroy. He spoke nervously out of the side of his mouth.

'Is he talking to us?' he hissed.

'Obviously,' whispered Leroy sardonically.

'W-why are we whispering?' said Kelvin.

'Good question,' whispered Leroy.

There was a tense moment as no one said anything. Marlon threw his voice over.

'Come on, man, this is invite only! I've been bigging you up!'

Kofi could feel his heart thumping in his chest. He had never imagined that this was why the olders would have invited them – to represent St Campions in a secret street rap battle. He glanced over at Kelvin, who looked a bit like a lost little Year 7 when his stutter took all his words. Kofi's confidence drained away.

A few murmurs of disapproval started to ripple through the crowd. One or two of the kids from other schools started jeering lightly. Marlon's face fell. His reputation was clearly on the line.

'You know what, come we go.' Leroy had snapped into life, his bravado turning on like a light switch. He strode towards the centre, a defiant scowl on his face, fist-bumping Marlon on the way. Kofi couldn't believe it. What was he going to do?

Leroy took a single deep breath and started rapping, pausing briefly before each line.

Straight out the gate, straight out of the school
And we pick it up like the five-second rule
Everybody's jealous cos I'm nobody's fool
You know that Coinboy and
the Reloader are cool . . .

Kofi couldn't believe it. Leroy powered on.

Listen up, everybody standing around
Three youngers and we're standing our ground
Marlon: we won't abandon the crowd
We make 'em look up like we
scrambled a pound . . .

When Leroy said 'like we scrambled a pound', he reached into his pocket, took out a pound coin and flicked it high into the air. It was an incredible move, full of confidence and style. Kofi was grinning from ear to ear. But his mouth fell open completely at what happened next.

Kelvin snatched the pound clean out of the air and stepped in, mid-flow.

Make you look up like we scrambled a coin,
All these other MCs are annoying
Campions: always bringing the noise
And we don't play like we've broken our toys . . .

Every face in the car park was now lit up, and everyone had gathered as close as possible around Leroy, Kelvin and Kofi. Marlon was bursting with excitement, hopping silently from foot to foot with a knuckle in his mouth, waving everybody quiet with his other hand. This was better than anyone had hoped. It was Leroy's turn to step back in:

Yeah we don't play like the playground is closed
Our lyrics stay fresh, like we're changing our clothes
Taking the stage like we're playing a role
A walk in the park, like we're taking a stroll . . .

And then Kelvin:

A walk in the park like we're flying a kite
I'm pulling the strings while you're trying to write

These other MCs will be crying tonight
When they realise that our rhymes are this tight

Back to Leroy:

Tight like a shoelace, tight like a knot
We light up a clash and you might have forgot
You do this a little, we do this a lot
So I don't have to prove that it's skills that I've got

Then Kelvin again:

It's skills that I got and it's skills that I show
The crowd says 'wow' and the crowd says 'whoa'
If you don't know, now everybody knows
We're the Campion boys and
we're running the show.

Kofi was loving it. Kelvin and Leroy were trading bars back and forth, building on each other's rhymes. By the time they were finished the crowd were completely won over, and Marlon was looking left to right with a happy, smug look on his face. Kofi felt his chest swell with pride. For his school, for his friends, for the amazing moment that he had just witnessed. The words fell out of his mouth before he knew it:

'And THAT'S how it's done!'

He stood between Leroy and Kelvin and draped his arms casually over their shoulders, pulling the kind of face you'd find on a rap album cover.

Yep. St Campions had *definitely* arrived.

10

Three's a Crowd

Over the next few weeks, the car park rap cyphers became the absolute, number one highlight of Kofi's week. Every Monday, Kofi would:

a) make sure that he didn't get history detention, and
b) go with Leroy and Kelvin to the secret spot.

Kofi was nowhere near as good a lyricist as Kelvin or Leroy, and Leroy had obviously been practising, so Kofi could only really join in by saying the rhyming word at the end of a line, hopping about while the other two went back and forth. Then the three of them would walk to the estate sharing a box of chips from the good chicken shop – the one that gave you free ketchup. It was a happy time, with the sun still out and the comforting sounds of the radio station welcoming Kofi on his way home through the estate.

It wasn't how Kofi had thought the year would go, but before long, he, Kelvin and Leroy were pretty much an inseparable trio.

Or so Kofi thought.

'What are you doing here?'

It was a Friday after school and Kofi had just been let out of science detention, for the third time that year. The school was quiet, with only a few teachers milling around and the corridors empty of kids. He'd spotted Kelvin's satchel at the entrance to the library and when he went to investigate, there was Kelvin.

Kelvin opened his mouth as if to reply. He looked sheepish, like he'd been caught out. In a short moment, Kofi discovered why.

From round a corner emerged Leroy. He wasn't what you would call a library kind of kid, so it was a big surprise to Kofi, seeing him there at all.

'*Leroy?*'

Kofi looked from one to the other and back again and put two and two together. They were hanging out, in the library. Kofi took a look at the pages in front of Kelvin and saw line after line of his unmistakably neat handwriting. They were lyrics.

'Oh,' he said.

Kelvin spoke first.

'Yeah, Kofi, we were just . . . we were just working out some new lyrics . . .'

'Without me?'

An awkward pause hung in the air.

Kofi looked at Leroy. 'Do you even *have* a library card?'

Mrs Wagg's voice carried through the air. She had one of those deafening whispers that only old librarians ever seem to have.

'Closing in ten minutes, boys!' she boomed quietly. 'Leroy, your jacket's in the usual place, pet.'

Pet? thought Kofi. *Usual place?*

'Yes, miss,' replied Leroy obediently.

'*Oh*,' said Kofi.

He chewed his lip. Leroy held up his handful of A4 paper.

'We just need to finish up this bit,' said Leroy awkwardly. 'You should come see, man . . .'

56

Kofi wanted to be involved, of course, but he couldn't help but think there was a reason that he had been excluded in the first place. He knew he wasn't anywhere near as good a rapper as his friends, but he never thought that they might end up working on things without him. It made him feel left out.

'No,' he began, 'I'll ... I'll go.'

Then more confidently: 'I need to get home for – something.'

The lie was unconvincing.

And with that he shouldered his rucksack and walked into the empty, echoing halls.

11

Uncle D's Good Advice

Back at the estate, it was already starting to get dark. It was the week after half-term, and the weather was changing. The low bass of the pirate radio station hummed in the background, but Kofi barely registered it, being so lost in his thoughts. It took three or four tries before he realised someone was calling out his name.

'*KOFI.*'

It was T, up at one of the first-storey walkways. Ever since Kofi had told T how to get free goes on the arcade machines they had become pretty good friends. Now that Mum and Dad knew that T wasn't a local badboy, they let Kofi go to his flat to play computer games too. It was an unlikely pairing, but it had become a genuine friendship.

T's friends Patrick and Edward were up there too, as usual, Edward with a cigarette candy stick in his mouth, as usual, and Patrick squinting at everything, refusing to wear his glasses, as usual. Kofi thought back to last year, before he knew them properly, and how scary he thought they were when they were hanging out. But now he knew that they were just ordinary kids like anybody else.

'Sup, man?' called T. 'You totally deaf now?'

Kofi wasn't in the mood for banter.

'No,' he said flatly. T grimaced slightly before carrying on.

'Well, listen, lemme know if you want to come round and play some Nintendo. I got *Killer Instinct* and it's wicked, trust me.'

Kofi would have usually jumped at the chance to play a new computer game, but not today.

'Maybe later,' he called up weakly.

'All right, safe,' replied T. And he melted into the shadows.

Five flights of stairs and Kofi was up at the flat, letting himself in.

'EEEEEEEEEEK!'

Before he knew what was happening, Kofi found himself wrapped in a pair of long, smooth arms, slightly less than suffocated by the smell of a flowery perfume. Then as quickly as it had started, the hug was over.

'Jeanette?'

His uncle's glamourous girlfriend was grinning from ear to ear.

'Look at you!' she squealed. 'My little Kofifi!'

At that point, a tall, dreadlocked figure emerged, smiling, into the corridor. It was Uncle Delroy.

'Yo!' he beamed, giving his nephew his second hug in two minutes. 'You getting big now, Kofi, innit!'

Uncle Delroy stood back to look at Kofi properly, flashing his gold tooth as his chains came to a rest around his neck. Kofi hadn't seen his favourite uncle in what felt like forever. A rush of joy flooded through him and he momentarily forgot all about what was going on at school, a huge smile spreading across his face. At that point, Emmanuel stuck his head out of the front room.

'Uncle Delroy and Jeanette have come to visit!' he said happily.

Then Gloria stuck her head out too.

'And he's getting us takeaway!'

She brandished two leaflet menus.

'Indian or Chinese?'

*

Before long, Kofi was walking back from the high street with Uncle D, carrying thin plastic bags full of takeaway boxes. His uncle was in good spirits, telling Kofi all about his recent adventures, but when they walked past Kelvin's block, Kofi became quiet. Uncle D could tell something was wrong.

'Wha'gwan, Kofi?' he asked, gently nudging his nephew with one shoulder. 'You don't feel like talking today?'

Kofi looked up at his uncle and opened his mouth to speak. Then he sighed.

'It's just some stuff at school,' he said eventually. 'One of my friends is … is …'

He paused, then decided to just be honest. It was only last year that he had spent weeks writing letters to his uncle where he told him everything. So he knew he could trust him now.

'My best friend is hanging out with someone else.

It's like they don't need me any more.' It sounded silly and childish coming out of his mouth, but it was how he really felt. He quickly explained what had happened with Leroy and Kelvin and their secret rap meetings. Then he looked sideways and down at the ground. Uncle D stopped walking.

'Listen up, Kofi,' he began. 'If there's one thing I know, it's that—'

'You're going to give me one of your gold chains?' said Kofi hopefully.

Uncle D kissed his teeth playfully. They carried on walking.

'If there's *one* thing I know about *you*,' he continued, 'it's that you can find a solution to *any* problem that comes your way. You're a natural businessman. The original *Coinboy*!' he added, shaking Kofi by the shoulder. 'I knew a few mandem like you from back in the day and trust me, they're doing *more* than OK. I know how this film ends.'

Kofi stopped in his tracks. He was staring into the middle distance, eyes wide in sudden concentration. It was what happened to him whenever a new plan hatched in his brain. *Film*, he thought to himself. *Film* . . .

'Uncle, what did you say?'

12

Kofi's Cunning Plan

The front room was all set and ready for the big takeaway feast. The little foldaway table was fully extended with chairs for everyone and Gloria had put the lamp on low, creating a lovely soft glow across the room. Mum and Dad were back from work and everyone was busy spooning food on to their plates, passing the little foil containers around.

While everyone ate, laughed and talked, Kofi quietly worked out the details of his new plan in his head. By the time the plates were cleared away and everyone had decamped to the sofas in front of the telly, he knew the next step of what he was going to do.

'Ooh, I LOVE this show!' said Jeanette, scooping up the remote and plonking herself down heavily on the three-seater, between Gloria and Kofi, making them bounce upwards slightly.

'*Family Fortunes*?' said Dad, looking back from the kitchen doorway.

Family Fortunes was a TV game show where families went head-to-head answering questions for prizes. You could play along at home. Kofi had always loved the sound effects when someone got an answer right or wrong.

'Yep!' enthused Jeanette, notching up the volume on the remote. 'Our survey says ...'

Everyone except Uncle Delroy responded instantly: '*BING!*'

Uncle Delroy looked around the room with a bewildered look on his face.

'Either you lot are watching too much telly, or I ain't watching enough ...'

'It's general knowledge, Delroy ...' warned Mum playfully, gliding towards the single-seater. 'You never did pay enough attention at school.'

'Cha!' retorted Delroy. 'Them teachers didn't have anything useful to teach a badboy like me.'

Gloria, Kofi and Emmanuel looked at him with raised eyebrows.

'But you lot make sure you study your books, yeah?' he added hastily.

'Look!'

Gloria was pointing at the telly. On the screen was a family of five, all smiling and waving at the camera.

'They're black!' said Kofi. You hardly ever saw black people on the TV, so it was a genuine surprise to see a whole black family on a Friday-night quiz show.

'You're right!' said Mum, standing up. 'I'll have to call Candice.'

'Sonia,' said Dad patiently, 'just because there's a black family on the telly it doesn't mean you need to—'

He stopped.

'That's Isaac that I used to work with at university!' he gasped. 'Call Auntie Vic, quick!'

The phone suddenly rang and Gloria dashed to pick it up.

'Hello?' Kofi heard her say. 'Yep, we know! ITV! Bye!' She slammed the receiver down.

'It was Auntie Pam,' she said breathlessly. 'Telling us to watch ITV.'

While all this was happening, Uncle Delroy looked around in confusion.

'All this for a *TV show*?'

'*Shhh!*' said everybody else.

The *Family Fortunes* host had blond hair and a plastic grin. He was ready with the first question.

'We asked one hundred people to name something you use ... to bake ... a *cake*.'

'Fork!' shouted Dad.

Mum looked at him sideways. 'So it's *university* you said you went to?' she said with one raised eyebrow.

'Flour!' said Jeanette, flicking her hair. 'Self-raising ideally, or one teaspoon of baking powder per cup of plain flour in equal parts ratio to sugar, butter and eggs.'

She realised everyone was looking at her in mild amazement, probably remembering how disastrous her attempts at cooking had been last year.

'What?' she said innocently. 'I've been practising.'

As *Flour* flashed up as the top answer, the final piece of Kofi's plan fell into place. He sprang to his feet and made for the kitchen. Everyone was totally engrossed in the TV so it was the perfect time to sneak off to the little store cupboard next to Gloria's room. Besides, they would just think he was going to the toilet. But he had to be quick.

Taking one final glance behind him, Kofi eased open

the cupboard door. It wasn't a big flat, so that was the main storage space for stuff that couldn't fit in the kitchen. He glanced past the camcorder, which had been placed carefully on the middle shelf, all wrapped up in its packaging.

Kofi's eyes searched briefly until he found what he was looking for.

BING! he heard from the front room.

There it was, among all the tins, tubs and bags. And it was the perfect shape and size.

Kofi grinned.

13

Two at a Time

'You brought a camcorder? To *school*?'

Kelvin's face looked almost exactly like a question mark as Kofi beamed proudly, holding his rucksack open to show his friends. Kelvin and Leroy spoke simultaneously.

'Why?' said Kelvin.

'Nice . . .' said Leroy.

'Why *thank* you,' said Kofi, tilting his head like a proud parent. He hadn't explained any of his plan yet but he already felt much better just having Kelvin and

Leroy's attention. Kofi naturally liked being right in the middle of things, even if it meant risking getting in trouble.

'It's my dad's,' he explained, lifting it out of his bag carefully.

'And he let you borrow it?' asked Kelvin in surprise.

'Not quite . . .' replied Kofi. 'But he only uses it every now and again and keeps it wrapped up the rest of the time.'

That much was true. Dad was only going to use the camcorder for church events, and nothing was lined up for weeks. Dad was super-excited about his new toy, but he was so busy, he only played with it on Wednesdays when he wasn't on late shifts. Besides, after all the initial excitement, Dad was the kind of person to leave expensive things alone, unless he really needed them. Dad was a creature of habit, so Kofi had already worked out that he wouldn't touch the camcorder at any other time, meaning that the coast was clear. The only problem was that Dad was always going into the storage cupboard for various bits and pieces, and every time he did he needed to move the camera box to one side. This meant that he'd know if the box was empty. But Kofi had thought of a solution. He leaned forward to explain.

'I replaced it with a sack of flour,' he said in a

conspiratorial whisper. 'So when he moves the box he'll think it's still there.'

Leroy was impressed. 'You're one sneaky yute!' he said with a grin.

The plan was simple. Kofi was going to use the camcorder to film segments of the weekly secret rap battles. At first he thought about getting Kelvin to just write out the lyrics from memory and make a new magazine, but he'd done that before and felt that he needed something new. A video series would be perfect. He could record from camcorder to VHS at home and sell them on to all the kids who weren't at the cyphers. You could get VHS cassette tapes at the pound shop, so the profit would come easy. It was a brilliant idea.

Kofi explained all this to his friends as they strolled towards the high street. It was Tuesday after school, and Leroy and Kelvin listened as Kofi talked excitedly, gesticulating wildly with his hands. Leroy was in straight away. He loved the idea of becoming an underground video star. Kelvin took a little longer to warm to the idea, but even he had to admit that it sounded like fun.

'Let's have a go then,' said Leroy as they approached the two-at-a-time newsagent's. Kofi knew that he should be careful, but he was happy to let himself get carried away. Even if Leroy was unpredictable. Kofi pulled the camcorder out of his bag and flipped it open, putting the viewfinder to his eye. He hit 'record'.

Leroy instantly started swaying around and playing up to the camera.

'Yo yo yo, whassup *baby*!' he said in a ridiculous American accent. The camera shook with Kofi's laughter. Kelvin looked left to right, wary and cautious. It didn't seem safe to be brandishing a brand-new, borrowed camcorder out in the streets like this, especially in school uniform.

By now the boys had reached the shop, Leroy talking to the camera like an American rapper while Kelvin looked on nervously. There were still more than a few kids milling around. Leroy cut through the crowd, walking backwards while Kofi kept the camera rolling.

'And yo yo yo, this right here is where we gets the hook-up on the *soda*, the *candy* and the *chips* . . .'

Like Leroy, Kofi had watched more than enough American TV to know the American names for fizzy drink, sweets and crisps. He giggled at the impersonation, keeping Leroy right in the middle of the viewfinder.

'So let's say whassUP to the homie Clapman one time . . .'

Leroy was getting completely immersed in his weird fantasy. He gave Clapman a pat on the shoulder and breezed into the shop, Kofi following closely. Leroy moved so confidently that Clapman was momentarily stunned and let them through, even though there were already two schoolboys in the shop.

Kofi had all his attention focused on Leroy's antics through the viewfinder, so he didn't notice what Kelvin had noticed, which was a group of St Campions kids filing into the shop behind Kofi and Leroy, pushing past a now very flustered Clapman. There was excitement in the air, but it was tinged with danger.

Inside, there was barely enough room to turn around with a rucksack on your back. The shop was stacked high with all manner of sweets, crisps and chocolates, with a huge wall of magazines and rows of brightly coloured fizzy drinks. Behind the counter was the ancient shopkeeper who never spoke and dropped the change into your hand from high up, like he was scared he might catch something from you. He looked up, alarmed. The shop was being swamped by St Campions shirts, ties and blazers. See, this was why it was two at a time.

Kofi noticed a semi-familiar face over by the shelves of drinks. It was an old man, shabbily dressed, who smiled at Kofi with a mouth that showed more gums than teeth. Kofi tried to remember where he had seen this man, but then he felt his left shoulder get jogged. Then his right shoulder. Then both shoulders at the same time. Before he knew what was happening he was surrounded. The shop was full.

'Please, please!' screamed the ancient shopkeeper in an accent that Kofi couldn't place. 'Two at a time!' It was the most he had ever heard him say.

Then everything happened in a blur:

An outsized rucksack knocked over a stand of greeting cards. A low jeer went up while jostling bodies started pushing each other. Mischievous hands started grabbing at chocolate bars and bags of crisps. A louder jeer went up. Eyes widened and mouths flashed into manic grins. Unspoken dares became unthinkable actions. Sweets entered pockets. Magazines off the shelves. Chocolates on the floor. In a word: mayhem.

Kofi suddenly realised what was happening and pulled his eye away from the viewfinder. Emmanuel had once told Kofi about a book he'd done at school called *Lord of the Flies*. It was about a group of schoolboys who got stranded on an island and ended up turning into savages. The scene around him reminded him of that. He had to get out.

Leroy had a weird look on his face. He was biting his

lower lip excitedly. He exchanged glances with Kofi, who honestly couldn't work out if Leroy was actually excited or worried or enjoying himself or what.

'Let's go!' mouthed Kofi in a panic.

Leroy nodded and they sped out of the chaos, through flailing limbs and past Clapman, who was hopelessly trying to get everyone out. Kofi grabbed Kelvin by the arm on the way. Kelvin spoke through gasps as they sprinted away from the scene.

'I don't think that w-was – a good i—'

'We know!' interrupted Leroy happily. He still had that wild streak that got him in trouble last year. After about a minute of full-pelt sprinting, they rounded a corner and leaned against a brick wall to catch their breath. They weren't being followed. The coast was clear.

'I knew … we – should – have – stayed at – the library…' breathed Kelvin, leaning forward with both hands on both knees.

'Fun though, innit!' laughed Leroy, breathing heavily too.

Kofi looked at his friend sideways, chest heaving, camcorder still gripped in his right hand.

Was it? he thought to himself. He really wasn't so sure.

14

Music Videos and Cappuccinos

It was a grey Saturday morning and Kofi had just reached the fifth floor after an exhausting climb, carrying two handfuls of bulging plastic shopping bags. The faint strains of a reggae rhythm could be heard from the radio station, bringing a tiny bit more sunshine to the estate. On Saturdays Kofi had to go with Mum into the market and was basically the unofficial bag carrier. He hated it on colder days like this one, when the thin plastic handles would slice into his fingers like razor wire as the bags became heavier and heavier with each step.

'Can't we just not eat this week?' he said with a wince, dumping the bags on the ground outside their front door.

'Careful!' gasped Mum. 'You'll bruise the plantain.'

Kofi pouted as he examined his aching fingers.

'Sometimes I think you love plantain more than you love me,' he grumbled.

'I do,' said Mum, retrieving her key from her purse. 'Let's get inside. You can help me unpack.'

Kofi half carried, half dragged the mass of bags in through the corridor and into the kitchen, letting them crumple to the floor with a final gasp. He looked up. Gloria was in there, busy stirring a mug of something at the counter next to a recently boiled kettle. There were bowls of milk, sugar and little brown grains scattered all over the counter. For the usually neat and tidy Gloria, this was a mess.

'What you doing?' asked Kofi curiously, leaning forward to dip his finger into a creamy-looking mixture.

'I'm making a *cappuccino*,' she replied, batting his hand away. Gloria was always trying out the latest new trends. She'd seen someone drinking a *cappuccino* on the telly and wanted to see if she could make the Italian chocolatey coffee drink at home.

'You're making a *cup of tea now*?' said Kofi. 'So why've you got the coffee out?'

Gloria rolled her eyes and pushed past him on the way to the front room, carrying a large cup of frothy hot liquid. The adverts were just finishing as Gloria settled into the single-seater, crossing her legs and blowing into her drink. Her favourite programme was about to start. It was *The Chart Show*.

'Kofi!' called Mum from the corridor. 'Have you got the cold stuff in the fridge yet?'

'Yes, Mum!' he lied, drifting towards the telly. *The Chart Show* came on once a week, on Saturdays. It featured all the latest music videos from the pop charts. It didn't have any live performances like *Top of the Pops*, but it was the only place to see new music videos, unless you had Sky or cable. And if you were lucky, you might get some hip-hop, R & B, reggae, house or soul: black music that you didn't hear much on the radio.

'How's your crappy-tea-no?' he asked his sister, perching on the edge of the three-seater.

She opened her mouth to answer but was interrupted by a voice from the screen that was saying something far more exciting.

'In today's *hip-hop* and *R & B* special . . .'

Kofi and Gloria looked at each other, eyes widening. They couldn't believe it.

'Tape!' they both shouted at the same time.

Kofi sprang to the TV cabinet and started rifling through various big rectangular VHS cassette tapes, looking for something to record over. The chance to get a whole new selection of hip-hop and R & B music videos, on tape, was too good to pass up.

'*Grease*?' said Kofi, holding up one cassette.

'Nah, that's a classic,' said Gloria. 'Keep going.' He kept looking.

'*The Snowman*?' he offered.

'Nah, we watch that every Christmas,' returned Gloria. Kofi rummaged again.

'*First Holy Communion* . . .' he read from an ancient label.

'No way, Dad would kill us,' said Gloria. 'Quick, it's starting!'

Kofi dived back in.

'Um . . . how about . . .' He held up a cassette in a thin cardboard sleeve. '. . . *Songs of Praise 1991* . . . ?'

Gloria thought for a second.

'That was when Emmanuel's school choir was on the telly, wasn't it?' she said.

'Yep,' replied Kofi. 'He talked about that for weeks.'

Pause.

'Let's tape over it.'

'Good idea.'

'*Kofi!*' Mum's voice cut through the air as he scrambled to load the cassette into the video player before pressing 'play' and 'record' at the same time. '*Shopping.*'

'Sorry, Mum,' he said, heading back to the bags of groceries and touching fists with Gloria along the way.

*

By the time Kofi had put the shopping away and Gloria had finished her cappuccino, the two siblings had successfully recorded the following music videos from *The Chart Show*:

'Motownphilly' by Boyz II Men

'Slam' by Onyx

'Remember the Time' by Michael Jackson

'Creep' by TLC

'Poison' by Bell Biv Devoe

'Cherish the Day' by Sade

'I'm Every Woman' by Whitney Houston

'What About Your Friends' by TLC

'Real Love' by Mary J. Blige

Kofi was already familiar with a lot of the songs, having been listening to Emmanuel's collection of tapes since last year. He'd also been listening to a lot more hip-hop on the local pirate radio station, which played the latest tunes once a week. Kofi had made a point of tuning in and plugging Emmanuel's headphones in so that he could listen in peace.

Now he was making his own video project, this was the first time he really paid attention to how much the visuals added to the music. Watching the videos on *The Chart Show*, he found himself mesmerised by the colours and movement, wondering where the camera would need to be to get those angles, and how to make everything look so bright and vibrant. He noticed how the performers would often look directly into the lens when they were rapping or singing and how they would dance and perform at the same time.

Hm . . . he thought to himself as the images flashed across the TV screen. It was definitely giving him ideas about what to do at the next cypher.

After a while, Kofi was totally engrossed, getting lost in a daydream about how good his video would eventually be, and how everyone would want a copy.

'You still watching this?'

Kofi looked away from the screen at Gloria's

interruption. He was on his second viewing of *the Chart Show* hip-hop and R & B special. He pressed 'pause' on the video player and looked up at his sister, blinking twice.

'I'm going to meet Shanice,' she continued breezily, scooping up her keys from the sideboard. 'Everyone's out, so don't burn the flat down.'

And with that, she was gone.

Kofi didn't waste any time. He waited just about long enough to make sure that Gloria was definitely gone, then he snuck to the cupboard to retrieve Dad's camcorder, making sure to put the decoy bag of flour in, just in case. Kofi had spent some of his savings on a pack of three camcorder cassettes from the electrical goods shop on the high street. They were smaller than normal VHS ones, and only ran for thirty minutes. He was already down to his last tape, which was hidden in a shoebox under the bunk bed he shared with his big brother. Kofi didn't really have a concrete plan yet for what to do with all his footage, but after watching *The Chart Show*, he knew he had to up his game. Tucking the little cassette into his rucksack, next to the camcorder, he set off with a bounce, out of the flat.

15

A Chase
Through the Estate

'Um, I d-don't think I can do that.'

Kelvin spoke hesitantly, looking up at his friend with a mixture of confusion and bewilderment on his face. Kofi was standing in a clearing next to the dilapidated picnic tables, his back to Kelvin, but his head turned round as far as it could go, to face him. He had both arms wrapped around himself in a tight bear hug, and his legs were fully crossed, having completed a spin on his heels, in the dust. He was breathing slightly heavier than usual. The dance moves had taken a bit out of him.

'It's easy,' he said, untangling himself and getting back into the first position. 'All you have to do is this ... then this ... then THIS, *this,* and finally ...'

He went through each step of the routine with sharp, deliberate moves. Kelvin was horrified.

'*This,*' finished Kofi, ending up in the back turn twist again. 'It's just like Boyz II Men do in their video. I thought you and Leroy could do it at the next cypher.'

If Kelvin's face came with subtitles they would have said *Are you crazy?* but his mouth didn't quite know how to catch up.

Kofi was just about to reach forward to hoist Kelvin up by the arms when a noise in the near distance made them both stop and look up.

DOOF. DOOF.

Kofi looked round, his head swivelling.

DOOF!

Car doors. More than one. And they were slamming.

Before Kofi had the chance to process what was going on, he heard a cry from one of the estate walkways up ahead. It was loud, and clear, and full of the unmistakable tones of fear.

'FEDS! *RUN!*'

Feds was the nickname that kids on the estate, and school, and the whole area as far as Kofi knew, used for the police. Now, both Kofi and Kelvin knew that they hadn't done anything wrong, so the police shouldn't be a problem, but they also knew that a police raid on the estate wasn't anything you wanted to be around for. Kofi could remember more than a few occasions when the police had ripped through the estate, looking for someone, or something. It had terrified him, how they would arrive in a flurry of cars and noise, stamping through the estate like an invading army. One time, he remembered peering through the fifth-floor window and seeing three or four police pinning some older boys from the estate up against a wall. It had scared him – the looks on their faces. He didn't want to ever end up like that.

Kofi looked at Kelvin with wide, unblinking eyes. Footsteps were pounding in their direction.

'Go!' he shouted, and both boys took off, Kofi hastily grabbing the camera along the way.

To anyone who doesn't know their way around, an estate is a total maze. But to Kofi this was his concrete playground, a habitat he had been exploring for as long as he could remember. People hanging out on the walkways, mainly kids, suddenly disappeared silently into their flats. There weren't many others about, but for anyone unfortunate enough to be further away from home, it was time to run. A few older kids were zigzagging in different directions, making their escape into stairwells. Kofi's heart was pounding as he thought frantically how best to get back to his block. He couldn't go the obvious way back because that was where the police were running from. Worse still, he realised, taking a brave glance over his shoulder, one of them had decided that Kofi and Kelvin were worth chasing.

Kelvin stumbled and fell sprawling to the ground. Kofi skidded to a halt and skipped back a step, hauling his friend to his feet and dragging him onwards.

'Oi!' a voice bellowed from behind. It didn't sound too happy about having to give chase, and the last thing you wanted to do was annoy a fed for no reason, but they had already started running. No way to turn back now.

'Through there!'

Kofi had spotted an alley gap that would lead Kelvin back in the direction of his block, round past the old bins. He bustled Kelvin through and paused to follow as Kelvin shimmied through the narrow space.

'Stop!'

The voice was louder, closer, and starting to sound angry. Kelvin was already out of sight. If Kofi went through now, the chasing policeman would be sure to follow. In a split-second instant, Kofi made a decision. A brave decision.

He ran in the other direction, leaving Kelvin free to get home. It was exactly what a good friend would do, and Kofi had made a decision to be the best friend that Kelvin had ever had.

Kelvin paused briefly as if wondering whether to come back, but Kofi urged him on, mouthing the word 'Go' with wide eyes. And with that, Kelvin slipped into the shadows. Kofi was on his own.

'*STOP!*'

The voice came from the other direction completely, making Kofi almost fall over as he swivelled his head to see. No way. It was *another* policeman. Kofi's head spun the other way and he took off at speed. He was totally innocent but he was starting to feel like he had actually done something wrong.

The rasp of Kofi's breathing mingled with the scuffling of his running feet. Images flashed through his mind of being slammed against the bonnet of a police car. His chest was starting to burn. He had to stop.

A shallow slope leading to a dark recess offered a welcome solution. Kofi skidded into the gloom. If he kept low, the police wouldn't even know he was there. It was dark, but it was a dead end, which made it safer. Maybe.

Out of nowhere, a fist suddenly gripped the front of Kofi's shirt with a powerful twist of fabric. Kofi gasped.

'*Got you.*'

16

Kofi and T's Great Escape

'You!'

T's face shone through the gloom of the underground car park. He put a finger to his lips and slowly released his grip on Kofi's top.

'This way,' he whispered, making sure to move as quietly as possible. The direction they were moving in was almost total darkness.

'I thought you were a fed,' whispered Kofi, gripping the camcorder tightly and trying to get his eyes used to the dark.

T looked down at him.

'Do I look like a fed?'

Fair point.

They were now deep underneath one of the blocks. The smell of dark oil, leaked from long-abandoned vehicles, was becoming more intense, and Kofi could feel a thick slipperiness underfoot.

'I used to play in these when I was a yute,' explained T as they crept deeper. The carcass of an ancient car sat like a fossil beneath a broken strip light.

'When was the last time you were in here?' whispered Kofi, disoriented.

'This far?' began T. 'Never,' he admitted. He turned to face Kofi. 'I've always been too scared.'

The sound of nearby scuffling made both boys stop momentarily. Kofi suddenly wished that he was somewhere else, glad that T was there, but terrified too.

The glare of a full-beam torch suddenly waved into view, casting impossible shadows across the greasy walls and low ceiling. They had been followed.

'Here,' muttered T, throwing his back against the nearest wall. They were trapped. The only way out was back in the direction of the light. With a lurch in his stomach, Kofi realised that it was over. And it was definitely going to be the worst trouble he had been in.

Even though Kofi knew he hadn't done anything wrong, he was terrified of what could happen if the police got involved. He remembered what had happened on the night Uncle Delroy was arrested – how the situation had so quickly gone from bad to worse, and how the police often didn't wait to ask questions.

The scuffling feet were getting closer. Kofi felt a tightening in his chest. Meanwhile, T was running his palms against the wall, looking for what exactly, Kofi had no idea.

CRUNCH!

There was a slight groan and Kofi felt the wall move.

'Help me, man,' said T through gritted teeth.

They pushed. Another crunch, and the wall lurched open. It wasn't a wall. It was a door. A door leading into a stairwell.

'Now!'

Kofi didn't have to be told twice. With a push, he leaned his full weight against the door. It opened just wide enough for both boys to slip through, then closed with a final groan.

'No way ...' said Kofi, talking mainly to himself as he looked around. 'But where are we?'

T's eyes lit up.

'Rah ...' he said in wonder. 'We're *in* the block. This

must be one of the service access areas behind the flats. I can't believe I've never found this before.'

T was excited, but Kofi could still feel the risk of danger. They were in a tight stairwell, barely lit by dim light bulbs in little steel cages. The air smelled stale and musty, and it was clear that no one had been there for quite some time. T pointed at the stairs.

'This way,' he said.

The only way was up.

'STOP. POLICE!'

The voice came from below them, booming like thunder into the stairwell, making Kofi's heart fall into his trainers. He looked up at T, whose face had suddenly melted into despair. They couldn't believe that the police officer had actually followed them this far. He must have been *RoboCop* or something. And they both knew that even though they hadn't done anything wrong, getting caught would not make for a happy ending to the story.

Just as the sound of heavy footsteps began to advance, a loud clang interrupted Kofi's thoughts. Both pairs of eyes swivelled in its direction. A small rectangle of daylight had appeared at the top of the stairs. In it crouched someone Kofi had never seen before. It was a man in big white high-top trainers and a baggy click suit. A click suit is a kind of patchwork tracksuit made of all different types of fabric, arranged in a haphazard pattern all over in a dazzling array of colours. Kofi had wanted one for as long as he could remember.

The mysterious figure gestured for the boys to approach. Kofi and T looked at each other and decided that going ahead was much better than heading back towards the police. They followed him silently.

The mystery man had a step in his high-top fade and a hand full of sovereign rings. Kofi lost all sense of time as they climbed through the concrete innards of the building, lit by dim bulbs, sometimes flickering in the gloom. Eventually the click suit stopped. He was in a half crouch, holding open a hatch that neither boy had realised was there. When he spoke, his voice was somehow raspy and nasal at the same time, hissing urgently but with a commanding sense of calm too. Kofi vaguely wondered if he had heard it somewhere before . . .

'Come, then.'

Kofi and T looked at each other. They didn't wait. Kofi taking the lead, they scurried up the final few steps and darted through the hatch.

17

A Meeting on the Roof

Kofi blinked into the daylight, followed by an equally bewildered T. Their mysterious helper crouched low at the hatch, busy fiddling with locks and clasps. Kofi saw him reach deep into his pocket and retrieve a screwdriver with a transparent handle, like one he'd seen his dad never use at home. After the stranger had secured the hatch with a final sharp twist, Kofi rose slowly to his feet and blinked twice. He could barely believe what he was seeing.

'Rah...' whispered T. Like Kofi, he was also spellbound.

Before them stretched a seemingly never-ending view of South London. Buildings jutted skywards in a jagged puzzle of concrete and stone, while roads criss-crossed below, oozing with traffic and people. Kofi could see as far as the library at the end of the high street, the clock tower glinting in the late afternoon sun. Even further, trains were snaking about above street level, while a flock of birds freewheeled into the clouds. They were on the roof of one of the estate blocks, and the view was breathtaking. Kofi instinctively raised the camcorder to eye height and pressed 'record', not once taking his eyes off the view. He panned slowly left to right, taking in the skyline as the little cursor blinked red.

'It's cool . . . innit.'

The mystery helper spoke in low tones, with a slight lisp. Kofi noticed that he stretched out the esses and didn't pronounce the tees, as though he was thinking about something else while he spoke. He was standing beside the two boys with one hand deep in his jacket pocket, the other stroking his goatee beard. He looked older than Emmanuel. Maybe around the same age as Uncle Delroy, but Kofi couldn't be sure.

The quiet held for a moment in the air.

'Who the hell are you, by the way?' said Kofi

suddenly, letting the hand with the camcorder fall to his side. He earned a sharp nudge in the ribs from T, who turned to him with a look that clearly translated as *Shut up, man, we need to get out of this alive.*

The man with the goatee paused and looked at Kofi through half-closed eyes. Kofi genuinely wondered if he was about to go flying off the roof.

'Nah . . . iss a good question . . .' said the goatee slowly, stepping forwards towards the edge of the rooftop to have a look below. He crouched down and steadied himself with one hand on the ledge.

'Linton . . .' he said finally, scanning the scene below.

Kofi was a naturally good judge of character. He wasn't picking up any danger signals from this mysterious saviour. So he took a few strides forward to join him.

'*Kofi,*' hissed T.

Kofi squatted next to Linton and leaned forward to see what he was looking at. Below, a scattering of police cars were sat like insects with their wings open, while groups of police officers milled around. Near a van, Kofi could make out a small group of kids from the estate circled by officers in black and white. He couldn't be sure, but it looked like they were in handcuffs. Linton kissed his teeth slowly.

'The boydem always messing with the mandem . . .' he rasped under his breath. 'Even the pickney . . .'

Kofi knew from his mother's side of the family that 'boydem' was Jamaican patois for 'the police'. 'Pickney' meant kids.

They waited in silence for a while longer. The police gradually returned to their vehicles and left the estate, taking the handcuffed youths with them in a slow-moving van.

'All right then,' said Linton, shaking his head, rising to his feet and dusting himself off. 'We're good.'

'So where to now, Lints?' said Kofi, dusting himself off too and turning the camcorder over in his hands. The older man looked at this strange little kid with a raised eyebrow, then turned to face T as if to say *Is he for real?*

'Um, don't mind him,' stuttered T. 'Thanks, man,' he continued. 'You really saved us back there.'

'Hey, do you live up here? Must be cold,' said Kofi. He had a habit of letting questions leave his mouth before he'd thought them through. 'I bet the pirate radio station will be starting up soon. I need to get home . . .' Kofi continued, thinking out loud.

Linton stopped.

'Pirate radio station?'

'Yeah,' replied Kofi, pointing in the general direction of his block. 'That's what my big brother, Emmanuel, says it is. I love it. You can tune in on the radio from all over the estate.'

Linton's eyes momentarily lit up.

'Come,' he instructed, heading towards another corner of the rooftop. T looked at Kofi, who gave him a half shrug. There wasn't any other way to get off the roof and Linton had been safe enough so far. Besides, Kofi was curious about whatever it was that their mysterious saviour wanted to show them.

'Coming!' he called excitedly. T rolled his eyes and jogged after them, hissing at Kofi to hold up.

In a matter of seconds, Linton took them to what Kofi hadn't realised was a little service door that led back down into the block, from further across the rooftop than the hatch they had escaped through. Linton thrust a hand into a different pocket and retrieved a long set of pliers with a red rubber grip. Kofi looked at the pliers, then at Linton, then back at the pliers.

'It's a key,' he lisped, with a smile, flashing a gold tooth out of the side of his mouth. 'Come on.'

The door yawned open, exposing a dark cavernous entrance with steps leading downwards. Another hand reached into another pocket and out came a torch.

Linton flicked it on and waved the light down into the dark stairwell. Kofi hesitated slightly as Linton stepped nimbly in.

'After you, man,' said T.

The journey back into the block should have been slow and careful, but Linton moved fast. Kofi and T had to almost stumble to keep up, and it took all their concentration not to fall, so conversation was out of the question.

Just as Kofi started to worry that he probably should have taken his chances scaling down the side of the building instead, Linton raised a sudden hand, signalling them to stop.

'What?' said T, in a mild panic. Kofi noticed that T was breathing heavily, and realised his own breathing was coming in quick, short rasps. It was tense. Linton tucked the torch under his arm and rummaged around in another pocket briefly, before producing a small, silver key.

'In here,' he said, turning the key in a small lock.

As if from nowhere, a door swung open. Kofi gasped.

In front of him was a flat, much like the one he lived in, but unlike anything he had ever seen before.

Everywhere he looked there were piles of complicated-looking machines with wires and cables trailing like jungle vines all over them. There were electronic devices that Kofi couldn't even have imagined, covered in little lights, knobs and switches. He let his eyes pan across the flat, trying to make sense of it all. The walls were almost completely covered in posters and flyers for club nights and live DJ events, with hundreds of names – some in huge letters and many more in tiny lines underneath. There were stickers and graffiti too, with names and tags that Kofi couldn't work out. He peered further in and saw countless milk crates scattered all over the floor, filled with records; more records than Kofi had ever seen in his life. Even more than he'd seen in Kelvin's mum's flat last year. A large wooden table by the doorway was dominated by two turntables and a massive desk of buttons and dials, as well as two large reels of what looked like video tape, just much, much bigger. The table had a drawer with a brass handle at the front and a deep, diagonal scratch, like a scar.

Elsewhere, microphones craned across the room on stands with crooked joints, looking a lot like black and silver scaffolding in this mad technological landscape. And finally, up by the big window were stacks of massive speakers, standing proud. They looked like they could be heard for miles around.

Linton stepped into the room fully and turned to face his two bewildered guests.

'Welcome to Clipper FM.'

18

The Secret Radio Station

'Wait, *you're* the pirate radio station?'

Kofi couldn't believe it. He'd been hearing music from this place for as long as he could remember. It had never occurred to him that he might one day actually see where it was coming from. And he could never have pictured a set-up like this. It was magical.

'Yeah, man,' replied Linton proudly. 'Just a likkle ting I inherited back in the day, innit.'

Kofi nodded slowly. He had no idea what Linton was talking about.

'Tea?'

Linton was holding a tin of teabags that he had retrieved from a cupboard up by the small window.

'*Yorkshire* Tea,' said Linton, shaking a bag out of the tin. 'The best cuppa in the world, bruv.'

'Yes, please,' Kofi replied. It had been a long afternoon.

'How does it all work … ?' murmured T slowly, soaking it all in.

'Well, you put those little bags in hot water and stir it with a spoon,' quipped Kofi. He couldn't help himself.

Linton laughed a low, dry chuckle.

'You're a funny yute, man,' he said, flicking a small electric kettle on. 'What's your name again?'

'I'm Kofi,' said Kofi. 'And this is T.'

Linton paused.

'*Coffee* … ? And *Tea* … ?'

His face broke out into a wide grin. The two boys looked at each other. Kofi had never once realised what their names sounded like. His mouth stretched into a smile.

'I guess you man *definitely* want a hot drink then,' laughed Linton, reaching for a couple of mugs. 'Lemme show you how it works.'

For the next fifteen minutes, Linton was like Willy

Wonka in *Charlie and the Chocolate Factory*, talking the boys through all the weird and wonderful secrets of his pirate radio set-up. He was an enthusiastic guide, even happy to answer all of Kofi's 'what does this do?' questions. T was mesmerised too. He loved technology and had a knack for understanding how different gadgets work.

'What's that red light for?'

Kofi was pointing at a heavy-duty-looking bulb in a little wire cage. A mischievous glint flashed in Linton's eye and his mouth fell open into a toothy grin. His voice lowered to a conspiratorial whisper.

'Ey, rudeboy, you wanna go *live*?'

When he said 'live' his eyes widened to show the whites all round and his eyebrows rose up high on his forehead. Kofi mimicked him unconsciously, grinning too. He didn't know what it meant, but it sounded exciting.

Linton started hovering over the equipment, switching buttons and flicking switches. Kofi had already forgotten what they were for. T watched intently. Then Linton reached into a nearby crate and withdrew a random 12-inch vinyl record with a blank white label. Kofi noticed that the crate had a piece of masking tape on it with the word 'Jungle' written in graffiti scrawl. Linton carefully placed the record on a turntable and lowered the needle with delicate fingers. Then he leaned to the right and pushed a red button with one hand, while flicking two switches with the other.

The red light pulsed into life.

Kofi jumped at the sound of the music as the record started playing. It was all clattering drums and a wobbly bassline, filling the flat with sound. Loud. Then the vocals kicked in. Kofi recognised it immediately.

'"Coinboy"!' he exclaimed.

'Wait, what? You know this tune?' replied Linton over the music.

'Yeah, man, it's my uncle! Dreaddy D!'

Linton pulled a quizzical face and looked at T for confirmation. T shrugged. Neither of them could have known that this was the song that Uncle Delroy had made last summer, accidentally inspired by Kelvin's poetry.

'Long story,' called Kofi, dancing with his hands and grinning. He'd never heard the song sound so good, on a proper sound system like this one. He started rapping along with his uncle's vocals, pretending to sway imaginary dreadlocks on his head. Both Linton and T were doubled up with laughter.

It wasn't long before Linton swung one of the microphones over to Kofi, pushing up a volume slider on the mixing desk as he did so. Kofi paused in his dance, hesitating at the invitation. Did he really want him to *say* something? On air? Meanwhile, T was busy rummaging around in the crates and selecting records to play. The music was booming, making it impossible to have a proper conversation. But Kofi didn't need words to see that T had found something special. With an excited gleam in his eye, the older boy slid a record out of a plain white sleeve and placed it on a turntable, ready to mix into the previous track, while Linton looked on like a satisfied teacher. With a deft flick of the wrist, T pushed the record into life.

Kofi's eyes grew round. He recognised it instantly.

'"It Takes Two"!' he beamed.

Linton made a rolling motion with one hand and pointed to the mic, as if to tell Kofi to carry on. Kofi was a DJ now. He knew the song well from one of Emmanuel's old cassette tapes. It was a hip-hop classic. He didn't waste any time.

'Yes, yes, people, you're listening to "It Takes Two" by Rob Base and EZ Rock, live and loud on . . . on . . .'

Linton chuckled and cupped a hand around his mouth to speak.

'Clipper FM,' he called over.

'CLIPPER FM!' echoed Kofi. Then the first verse started. Or rather, it should have started, but there were no vocals. T slapped his palm against his forehead. He'd put the record on the wrong side. It was the instrumental version by mistake.

Kofi didn't miss a beat.

I'm gonna rap right now! I've got
ALL the style in this town!
I won't stop until I get known and I've
got more rings than a telephone!

They weren't the proper lyrics, but Kofi had made up his own words with Gloria, listening to the song over and over again with her when they were little.

He carried on enthusiastically while T selected another record and Linton showed him how to mix it in. All thoughts of the police and the chase that had led them to this discovery had completely left Kofi's mind. His whole world was the sound of the speakers, the records, and the fun he was having in this place that he'd heard, but never seen. He looked up as he came to the end of the verse and Linton was giving him the thumbs-up while T had one hand on a record, the other on one ear of the headphones he was wearing. Kofi's grin stretched from ear to ear.

*

'I'm not gonna lie; you lot was very good on the radio, you know . . .'

Linton spoke with a lazy drawl as he leaned against the door frame of the flat's front door. He was holding a fresh cup of tea with the other hand deep in a trouser pocket. It was just starting to get late and there were a few streaks of orange in the sky. The pirate radio session was over and Kofi and T were in the walkway, getting ready to leave.

'Oh, don't forget this, innit,' said Linton, turning and taking a few short steps back into the flat. He returned with Kofi's camcorder, holding it out in front of him. 'Be careful with that. It looks new.'

'Oh!' exclaimed Kofi. He looked up to the sky and did a quick sign of the cross in celebration. 'Thanks, man.'

'Yeah, thanks, man,' said T, touching fists with Linton.

'Iss all good, bredrin.' Linton nodded. 'Make sure you get back to your block safe, innit.'

'We will,' said Kofi with a grin. 'And make sure you play some hip-hop at about four thirty every day, when I'm coming home from school.'

Linton laughed. 'I will, man, I will.'

Kofi powered ahead. 'I've got a friend who would LOVE this. He's a rapper, like me. They call him Kels the Reloader. Best rapper at my school. He lives in that block over there.'

Linton raised an eyebrow. 'Swear down? Ey, bring him along some time. It's been good having you two here.'

Then he paused briefly and a serious look cast over his features.

'Don't tell no teachers or nothing where this place is, yeah?'

Linton looked genuinely worried. Kofi felt his face mirroring Linton's concern.

'Cross my heart,' he said, relaxing into a grin. 'I'm good at keeping secrets.'

Linton was visibly relieved. For some reason, he instinctively trusted this kid. With a final spud of the fists, the door closed and Kofi and T were left alone on the thin walkway. They started making their way towards the stairs.

'That was amazing!' yelled Kofi out of the blue. 'I

can't believe that *this* is where the pirate radio station has been all along.'

'I can't believe you were rapping on air,' laughed T. 'That was the bravest thing I've seen all day.'

'Hey, how can I help it if I'm going to be a Clipper FM legend,' joked Kofi. 'They'll be listening out for me across the *whole*—'

And right when Kofi said the word 'whole', five separate things happened:

He threw his arms open wide, gesturing to the *whole* estate, as per his previous sentence.

The little Velcro strap on the camcorder decided to unstick itself from itself.

The strap came completely loose from Kofi's right hand, which up until that point was cupping the camcorder safely.

Kofi's right hand waved directly over the top-floor-balcony edge.

The camcorder took one last desperate look at Kofi, then fell towards the ground.

Kofi's blood ran cold as he realised what had just happened.

The two boys looked at each other in horror before leaning forward with both hands on the balcony railing. They got there just in time to hear the camera go crack against the concrete below, a dark smudge against the pale grey. T looked at his horrified partner, whose face was now covered with both hands.

'How much did you say your dad paid for that again?'

19

'Go and Get Me a Ribena'

'... All the washing-up for the next six weeks, I get the remote *whenever* I ask for it, and *you* clean the bathroom instead of *me* until *your* next birthday.'

Gloria finished her list of demands and stood with her arms folded and her head cocked at an angle. Kofi opened his mouth in silent protest, extending both arms desperately. Gloria interrupted before he had a chance to beg.

'You're in no position to negotiate, Kofi,' she began, pointing at her brother with a laser-like finger. 'Have you seen the state of that thing?'

She pointed towards the table at the camcorder. Miraculously, it had survived the fall from the top floor, but there was clear damage and scuff marks along one side. Worst of all, the little door for the cassette wouldn't close at all. As Gloria pointed, the door crumpled open as though it had finally given up all hope. Kofi winced and fell to his knees in solidarity.

'I'm in so much trouble . . .' he whispered to himself, covering his face with his hands. Gloria crouched down and put her arm tenderly around his shoulder.

'Kofi,' she said softly. 'I don't care. Now go and get me a Ribena.'

Kofi looked up at his sister with a face of pure horror just as the front door clattered open. It was Emmanuel. They heard him taking off his coat and dropping his keys on the side as he came through the hallway. He was saying something about Mum needing something done by a certain time. Kofi swivelled sharply to look at Gloria. She returned the look, and without speaking, grabbed the battered camera and slid it into Kofi's open rucksack.

Emmanuel entered the room just as Gloria collapsed into the three-seater, putting both her feet up on the glass coffee table.

'Hey,' she said casually to Emmanuel, extending her palm in Kofi's general direction.

'Remote, please.'

Kofi looked up at the ceiling.

20

Let's Talk Business

The next few days went from bad to worse.

Bad: The police raid had extended way beyond Kofi's estate, which meant that the car park cyphers were well and truly over. It was just too risky to meet in big groups.

Bad: This meant that Kofi's big plan to make videos to sell to the rappers simply couldn't happen – and he hadn't thought of any other way to make the money he now needed to replace Dad's camera.

Bad: Kelvin was less than sympathetic about the

whole thing. His general conclusion was *I told you so*, which didn't help Kofi at all. And it was annoying too, because it was true.

Worse: Dad and Emmanuel had an event coming up at church, meaning that Kofi only had a matter of weeks to magic a replacement camcorder out of somewhere. The good news was that Dad had extra shifts at work, so he was too busy to play with the camera at all – and the novelty had worn off by now too. But time was still running out. Fast.

'You screwed up big time, bro,' laughed Leroy through a mouthful of crisps.

The three boys were walking along the high street after school. Kofi was trying to figure out ways of making the money he needed in the short time he had left and thought that maybe his two friends could help. It wasn't going very well. Kelvin was mainly shrugs and judgement, while Leroy was just finding the whole thing hilarious.

'Do another *Street Fighter* tournament, man,' said Leroy, licking his fingers.

They strolled past the two-at-a-time newsagent's and Leroy gave a cheeky salute to the shopkeepers inside. The shopkeepers scowled back at him.

'That didn't end so well . . .' said Kelvin.

'True,' said Leroy and Kofi at the same time. Leroy shrugged.

They walked in silence for a moment, remembering what had happened the year before. Kofi had to give back all the money they'd made to the minicab office, because it was their arcade game. That was also the night that Leroy confronted Kofi in the streets and Uncle Delroy got arrested.

'KOFI!'

All three boys looked up in the direction the voice had boomed from. It was coming from the top-deck window of a bus that had just pulled up at a red traffic light. Kofi cupped his hand over his eyes and squinted up.

'Shanice?'

His sister's best friend was leaning out of the window at the back, where the rudeboys and rudegirls sat. She was waving him up.

Kofi looked at both of his friends in turn, before sprinting off to the open platform before the lights turned green.

'I'd better g-go with him,' mumbled Kelvin, pulling his satchel tighter over his shoulder and setting off at a jog.

'Ey, wait for me, man!' sprayed Leroy, following suit.

They jumped on the platform just as the bus started to pull away.

Upstairs on the bus was the usual after-school set-up: a few civilians sat in the first few rows, then a few gaps of empty seats, then a scattering of kids filling up the back, sprawled over the double seats and eating junk food.

Rudegirls, Kofi thought to himself as he swung his way to the upper deck. It was all girls from St Ursula's, the same school that Gloria went to.

Shanice was square in the middle of the furthermost seat. She was holding court, patting the curls flattened across her temples and chewing theatrically on a piece of bubble gum. Kofi, Kelvin and Leroy were stood up, holding on to the overhead bar as the bus lurched into motion.

'Sup, ladies,' said Leroy, leaning forward confidently. 'Rah, Kof, your friends are *fit*.'

Shanice scrunched up her eyes and pulled her face back into her neck. 'Anyway,' she said, waving her hand dismissively. 'We need to talk.'

The bus lurched suddenly and the boys almost fell over.

'Sit down, man, innit,' said Shanice, brushing off the crumbs from Leroy's open crisp packet.

'My old business partner,' explained Kofi to Leroy as he sat down next to Shanice. Leroy chose a seat beside one of Shanice's friends with a high ponytail, winking at her as he sat. She rolled her eyes. Another friend with big hoop earrings patted the empty space next to her, inviting Kelvin to take a seat. He blushed visibly.

'How's it going, Kelvin darling,' asked Shanice in a sweet voice. 'I've missed you, babes.'

Kofi realised that these girls seemed to really like Kelvin for some reason.

'Hey, how come you never talk to me like that?' he asked.

'Shut up,' replied Shanice. 'I got a question for you.'

Leroy was laughing into his fist and trying to put an arm around the back of the seat.

'What is *this*?'

Shanice was holding a transparent plastic cassette tape in one hand.

'Uh, a cassette tape?' said Kofi unhelpfully.

Shanice's eye roll lasted a full four seconds. She kissed her teeth and produced a Walkman from her blazer pocket. After sliding the cassette into the little door, she clicked it shut and pushed 'play', cupping her hands around her headphones to amplify the sound.

Everyone leaned in.

Leroy's eyes widened into two saucers. He was the first one to speak.

'So you wasn't lying ...?' he gasped in wonder, turning to check with Kelvin that this wasn't some crazy dream.

Out of the speaker came the sound of someone talking and laughing, and then rapping, while a hip-hop record played in the background. It was quiet, with no bass, but you could make out whose voice it was, clear as day. It was Kofi's: from his afternoon with Linton on Clipper FM last weekend.

Shanice clicked the 'stop' button. 'I record Clipper FM every week,' she began, stuffing the Walkman back into her pocket. 'How is a picky-head yute like you getting on pirate radio though?' She chewed her gum furiously. 'I need answers.'

'I *told* you!' said Kofi, pointing a finger at Leroy and Kelvin in turn. Leroy still looked in a mild state of shock. Kelvin put both hands up and made a face.

'I b-believed you!' he said. 'I just thought you w-were exaggerating.'

'I've never exaggerated in my whole entire life!' exaggerated Kofi.

'Oi!' interrupted Shanice. 'I was *talking*? How did you get on Clipper? I mean, *god* knows why you were up there spitting them dead bars in the first place, but for real, I know bare man that would pay good money to spit on pirate radio, like all them man that used to go pitches and the car park and that and . . .'

She trailed off. Kofi was looking at her; his mind was clearly spinning.

'What?' she said, leaning backwards apprehensively. 'Why you looking at me like that . . . ?'

But before she could finish, Kofi had surged forward and wrapped his arms around her in the most massive hug.

'Ugh, man!' protested Shanice, pushing him away.

'You all right, bro?' laughed Leroy.

The bus swung round a corner on the approach to the Junction. As it swerved, the girl next to Kelvin sidled closer to him with a little giggle. He blushed and struggled to find somewhere to look.

'Shanice,' beamed Kofi, ignoring everyone else, 'I think you might just have saved my life. Let's go to the food court. Chips are on me.'

21

New Plans

'OK, so explain that again but this time try making some actual sense, yeah.'

Kofi, Leroy, Shanice and her two friends, Tanya and Janelle, were sitting at a table in the brightly lit food court, sharing a few small portions of fries. It was still that after-school zone where lots of kids in uniform were out and about. The Junction was the most popular hang-out spot and it was getting dark outside, so there was a lively buzz inside.

Kofi lowered his head and put his hands out parallel in front of him, edges touching the tabletop.

'*Subs*,' he said slowly. 'I don't know exactly what they are, but I've heard that people pay them to join a club or be part of an ...' He struggled for the right word, cycling his hands momentarily.

'... *organisation*.'

It was a concept that had been introduced to him by his big brother, Emmanuel. Shanice raised an eyebrow.

'So you think normal people will pay these – *subs* – to get on Clipper FM?' she asked, chewing a chip thoughtfully.

'I know it,' replied Kofi. In the back of his mind, he wondered if inviting a bunch of random rappers to Linton's radio station was a good idea, but the thought was instantly pushed aside by how genius his scheme was. Besides, Linton *had* said that it was OK to bring Kelvin along ...

'I think that sounds like a plan,' said Leroy, taking a chip. 'And while you lot are out rounding people up, me and Tanya will be at the cinema getting to know each other.'

'No we ain't,' replied Tanya, twisting her face into something between a scowl and a smirk. Then she turned and softened into a smile.

'I'd rather go with Kelvin anyway,' she simpered.

Kelvin spluttered on the can of cola he was drinking.

'Half the guys from the cyphers are here right now,' continued Kofi. Looking around, he could spot more than a few familiar faces already.

'Come on, what d'you say?' he said with a glint in his eye. He rubbed his thumb and forefinger together, indicating money. Kofi knew that he wouldn't be able to get anyone to sign up without Shanice's help, and he was willing to pay some of the profit for it.

Shanice couldn't help but smile. She had to agree; it was a pretty good idea.

'Come we go,' she said finally.

'Yes!' said Kofi, grinning. He stood up, rubbing his hands together.

As everyone got up to head off into the crowds, Leroy put a hand on Kelvin's shoulder to hold him back for a second.

'Kelvin,' he said with a serious expression on his face. 'Why do the girls think you're so cute?'

Kelvin paused, and shrugged.

'Probably because I am,' he smiled.

*

Over the next half hour or so, Kofi put every human effort into telling all the kids from the cyphers and clashes about this new opportunity to be on the secret radio station. Truth be told, he was just playing wingman to Shanice. He marvelled at how persuasive she was, able to pretty much just tell people to come along. It was like she was everyone's older sister the way she issued instructions, and it helped that she was naturally popular: people seemed to agree with whatever she said. As they drifted from group to group, Kofi found himself getting more and more excited at the prospect of getting all these rappers up in the top-floor studio. He didn't let himself worry about the fact that he hadn't yet asked Linton if it would be OK. He would get to that later.

Soon enough, they had a long list of names of all the kids who wanted to spit bars on Clipper FM. Shanice insisted that everyone put down a name of their choice, so there were some crazy rap names that had been made up on the spot. Things like: *MC Vybez, D-Money, Picksey, Triple T, Wrighter, Joka, Block Star, Ryu Spitter* and *Little Scrimmer*, to name a few. Kofi knew that he could get loads more at school the next day too.

It was mainly boys, but there were a couple of girls too, encouraged along by Shanice's easy confidence. Kelvin had been drafted in to write the actual list down, which he did in his little red notebook. Shanice and Kofi had decided that five pounds would be a good amount to ask for and most of the rappers were enthusiastic enough to promise that they would get the money asap. A few even paid up straight away, earning a little tick next to their MC name.

Looking down at the list, Kofi did some quick maths.

'There's more than forty quid here already . . .' he said in mild wonder.

Leroy whistled. 'I'm on for free though, yeah? Seeing that I'm helping with the set-up.'

'Who even are you anyway?' said Shanice dismissively.

'You're so rude, man!' laughed Leroy, to which Shanice blew him an ironic kiss, with an added eye roll for good measure.

Kelvin looked at his watch. 'I n-need to get back,' he said quietly to Kofi. 'My mum will be wondering where I am.'

Tanya gave a muffled squeal, placed one hand on her heart and bit the knuckle on the other. 'Can I keep him?' she asked Shanice.

'OK, meet here tomorrow, after detention?' asked Kofi, handing the red notebook back to Kelvin.

'I don't get detentions,' replied Shanice, extending an arm for a handshake. As Kofi went to shake it, she pulled it away sharply and gave him a slap around the back of his head instead.

'I haven't forgotten,' she said with a point of the finger. 'Come we go. My feet are tired.'

'Forgotten what?' called Kofi as she walked away with her friends. But she was gone.

'Link up later, yeah!' Leroy called after Tanya. Tanya turned and put two fingers in her mouth in the internationally recognisable symbol for *yuck*.

The boys started walking in the direction of the bus stop.

'Right then,' said Kofi, looking at Kelvin and Leroy in turn. 'You ready to be on the radio?'

22

The Big Day

On Saturday, Kofi could hardly wait to get out of bed. It was the day he had agreed with Shanice to meet with all the rappers who had signed up. The list had grown to well over forty names, so the plan was to organise them into three groups. At five pounds each, it was looking like seriously good money, and that was just for the first month's subs. Kofi was certain that he would soon have enough to replace Dad's camcorder, especially if he added all of his savings.

Kofi rolled quietly out of his bottom bunk, leaving

Emmanuel snoring softly on top. As usual, Kofi was the first one up. Normally he would turn on the telly and watch all the early morning cartoons, but he was too excited. He still wasn't worried that he hadn't yet told Linton about the subs. He was sure that Linton would be OK with it, and besides, he and Shanice had agreed to give him some of the profits. It'd be fine.

He took a step into the hallway en route to the bathroom and suddenly found himself face-to-face with his sister.

'What are you doing up so early?' he asked in a whisper, genuinely surprised. Gloria liked to sleep in on a weekend. She replied instantly.

'Kofi, I know all about your radio station plan – Shanice tells me everything.'

Kofi's mouth fell open slightly.

'You're not going to tell Mum and Dad, are you?' he pleaded. It was the last thing he needed.

'No, Kofi, I'm not going to tell Mum and Dad,' she said. 'But I am coming with you though.'

It wasn't a request. Kofi sighed.

'Fine,' he said. 'After I get back from shopping with Mum.'

'And make my breakfast and clean the bathroom . . .' Gloria added.

Kofi remembered their agreement and winced.

'Love you too, sis,' he said sarcastically.

*

Four hours, one shopping trip, and one reluctantly cleaned bathroom later, Kofi was finally ready to get on with his day. Dad was at work, Emmanuel was at his weekend job at the second-hand furniture shop, and Gloria was sprawled in the living room 'doing coursework' in front of the TV. Mum was finishing up sorting out the whole flat before she went to meet Auntie Pam. She'd already agreed to let Kofi go and play with Kelvin, as long as he didn't get into any trouble, of course. She was firing instructions at random while she hovered from room to room.

'Gloria – make sure the stew doesn't burn.'

'Yes, Mum.'

'Kofi – don't use the new bread if you make a sandwich.'

'Yes, Mum.'

'And don't forget your key if you go out.'

'No, Mum.'

'Are you listening to me, Kofi?'

'Yes, Mum.'

And so on. But before long, she had given them both a peck on the forehead and, closing the door behind her, was gone.

Kofi and Gloria waited a few minutes until they were sure that Mum would be down the stairs and well on her way. Then they gave it a bit longer in case she stopped to talk to Mrs Weaver on the way down. Then the sibling telepathy kicked in and they both jumped up. Gloria clicked off the TV.

'Let's go,' she said, leaning into the kitchen to turn off the stove. Kofi could tell she was excited by what the afternoon had in store. Going to a pirate radio station with a bunch of paying rappers was definitely better than doing coursework in front of the telly.

'Remember, Gloria, this is MY plan,' he reminded her.

She scowled at him. 'Remember, *Kofi*, I can tell Mum and Dad any time I want.'

Kofi mimicked her in a high-pitched silly voice and ducked to avoid the cushion that she immediately threw at his head.

'Come on,' he laughed, grabbing his jacket. He was in a good mood.

*

It was a clear, crisp afternoon and the sun shone down brightly on the two siblings as they walked. The estate was humming with the usual sounds – bikes been ridden by back-pedalling kids, a few dogs barking – with some kids hanging out and people going about their business. Kofi had arranged to meet at the dilapidated picnic tables between his and Kelvin's block. Shanice had promised to be ready with all the radio hopefuls, and Kelvin would be there with his notebook to take names.

'Admit it,' said Kofi, skipping with his hands in his pockets. 'You're impressed.'

Gloria tutted. 'I'm impressed with how stupid you are. I mean, you're lucky to be getting away with this—'

They turned a corner and stopped in their tracks.

'At all ...' Gloria trailed off. Kofi gasped.

In front of them was a scene they couldn't have possibly imagined. There must have been sixty, maybe seventy people milling around in groups, teenage boys and girls decked out in their best streetwear. Some were standing in small circles, rapping in cyphers, others on their own reading through pages of handwritten lyrics. Many were just socialising casually, sipping cans of fizzy drink or munching on chocolate bars. It looked like a carnival without the rides.

'I thought you said about twenty?' said Gloria.

'I did!' replied Kofi.

As they drifted through the crowd, Kofi could hear snatches of lyrics being practised and recited out loud. He recognised a handful of faces from older year groups at school, and a few more from the pitches during the summer, but most of them were too busy concentrating to bother trying to say hello.

Out of nowhere, the hoop-earring-ed, long-fingernailed figure of Shanice came cutting through the crowd, heading straight for Gloria and Kofi. Her eyes were wide, but there was definitely something like a smile trying to break out on her face.

'Hey, girl!' she said to Gloria, greeting her with a kiss on each cheek. Kofi cut in.

'Who are all these people?' he exclaimed.

Shanice did a half shrug and began patting the curls on the side of her head.

'People brought friends,' she said nonchalantly. 'I made it sound wicked, innit. Anyway, I'm sure you can explain to the DJ that we have a few extras. He's expecting a crowd, right?'

Kofi started chewing his lip.

'Right?' repeated Shanice.

Kofi suddenly became very interested in a little

pebble next to the toe of his left trainer. Shanice grabbed him by the shoulders.

'Oh – my – *days* . . .' she said, the realisation dawning slowly. 'Don't tell me you didn't tell him . . .'

Kofi swallowed. 'I didn't tell him.'

'Kofi!' said Gloria and Shanice in unison. They couldn't believe he would set all this up and not tell the radio station in advance.

'Are you crazy? What if we get there and he tells us to go away?' Gloria was horrified. Shanice was dusting her hands and shaking her head.

'Your brother is a *proper* eediyat,' she said. 'I'm done with this yute. You do realise half of these people have paid up front? What the hell are we telling them?'

'Relax!' said Kofi with a slight crack in his voice. He hadn't considered that not telling Linton would be such a big deal, but now Shanice and his sister had reacted like that, the fear was starting to grip him. 'Linton will be cool with it, I swear.'

His voice even sounded unconvincing to himself. 'Trust me?'

At that point, Kofi spotted the small figure of Kelvin appearing from the other side of the tables. He took the excuse to leave his sister and business partner to their teeth kissing and eye-rolling and ran off in Kelvin's direction.

'I – I didn't get all these names ...' began Kelvin uncertainly, looking around at the buzzing crowd.

'Don't worry about that now,' Kofi said, glancing over his shoulder. 'We'd better start praying that Linton lets us in.'

Kelvin's eyebrows jumped to the top of his head. 'You mean you didn't tell him yet?'

'Oh, don't you start,' Kofi replied. 'You got your notebook?'

Kelvin produced it from his satchel. Kofi nodded and took it from his hands, opening it up to the most recent page. He looked at the names. Then he looked up at the crowds. Then back to the names. Then to the crowds again. Kelvin saw the mild beginnings of panic start to flutter in Kofi's eyes.

'Shanice!' Kofi called back to where he had just come from.

'New plan,' he said to Kelvin.

23

Heading to the Top

It took a short while, but between Kelvin's notebook, Shanice's incredibly loud voice and Gloria's organisational skills, the crowd was soon split into three groups: the group who were lined up and paid up to go and spit bars on Clipper FM; the group who had turned up out of the blue and would come back another day; and the group of hangers-on who were just looking for something to do.

Somehow, Shanice had managed to persuade groups two and three to shuffle out of the estate and head somewhere else for the afternoon, leaving about fifteen MCs in group one ready and waiting for their moment of glory, live on air. The wait had done nothing to squash the levels of excitement. If anything, the rappers were getting even more energised as they got closer to the big moment.

'You best hope Linden lets us come through,' whispered Shanice to Kofi as she sat, arms folded, on the edge of a picnic table.

'Linton,' corrected Kofi.

'Whatever, man,' said Shanice breezily. 'These lot are ready, alie.'

'Alie,' echoed Gloria.

Kofi rolled his eyes as the two girls walked off into the crowd, leaving him standing next to Kelvin.

'She's right though,' said Kelvin, after a pause.

Kofi pouted.

The sound of Shanice's voice cut through the air. 'All right!' she shouted, flipping through a few pages in Kelvin's notebook. 'Cray-Z, Nykee Sprint, Saracen P, Barz Kid, Ryu Spitter . . .'

She paused to look at Gloria and shake her head.

'. . . E Zee, Young B, Tiny B, Little B and . . . Bay . . . Baybee B? All right, one of you lot is gonna have to change one of these Bs into something else, man. Let's go.'

An excited buzz went up among the crowd. Shanice pointed at Kofi. 'Follow him.'

Suddenly, Kofi felt a wave of dread wash through his chest. He hadn't stopped to let the full reality of the situation sink in: that he had set up a whole bunch of promises that he might not be able to keep. He felt his face flux through a range of emotions, resting into the most awkward of smiles.

'This way!' he said in a too-loud voice. Then he turned and began walking. Kelvin fell into step beside him.

'Are you s-sure Linton even exists?' Kelvin whispered through a small smile.

Kofi rubbed the back of his neck. 'I hope so.'

He led the train of rappers into the estate and up towards Linton's block. The walkways were quiet, and as Kofi walked, it dawned on him that everything was quiet. Too quiet. The muffled bass of the pirate radio station, usually pulsing like a heartbeat through the concrete, was ... not there. Something was wrong.

They reached the bottom of the block that housed Linton's flat. Two of the Bs were in a heated discussion over who should get to keep the initial. They had decided to battle it out on air, which had proven to be a popular idea among the other rappers.

'It's on the top floor,' interrupted Kofi, wondering seriously if he should make a run for it. 'I'll go up first.'

Like every block of flats Kofi had ever been in, the steps up to Linton's flat were long and dark, with faint smells of things that you didn't want to linger around for too long. Eventually, they reached the top floor, spilling into the narrow walkway. The sun was hanging low, and an orange glow was ushering the transition from afternoon to evening. A few pigeons that were resting on the balcony flapped wildly and fluttered off into the sky. Kofi peered as far as he could down the walkway before advancing slowly. He reached the door to the flat and turned to address the crowd. Something wasn't right.

Knock knock knock!

Kofi rapped his knuckles against the door three times in quick succession. Nothing. Gloria and Shanice excuse-me'd their way to where he was standing. He tried again.

Knock knock knock!

Pause.

Nothing.

Again.

Shanice was now pinching the bridge of her nose between a forefinger and thumb. Before Kofi could raise his fist to try for a third time, Gloria's voice stopped him short.

'No way . . .' he heard her say quietly to herself.

She was by the window further down the walkway. It was one of those reinforced ones made out of that glass with the criss-cross wire running through it. Gloria looked up, biting her bottom lip.

'Guys,' she said slowly, 'I think I've found something.'

24

Bad News on the Top Floor

Kofi, Shanice and Kelvin crowded around Gloria to have a closer inspection at whatever it was she was looking at. It was a piece of paper, slightly bigger than A4, stuck fast to the plaster beneath the window with some kind of plastic wrapping. The lettering was bold and clear. Gloria started reading aloud:

'Notice of ... *eviction* ... This property is to be ... vacated, effective immediately ... blah blah blah ... until the tenant or tenants are legally permitted to ... return.'

She turned to face everyone. 'It's empty.'

'Are you *kidding* me?' said Shanice, splaying the fingers of both hands in frustration. 'What do we tell that lot?'

She thumbed in the direction of the rappers. One of them caught her eye and strode over. It was Ryu Spitter.

'Which lot?' he pouted, folding his arms. 'What's going on, man? This don't look like no radio station to me . . .'

Ryu cupped a hand over his brow and leaned forward to peer into the dark window.

'Ey, you man . . .' he continued, calling one of the Bs over. 'Is this place even, like, open?'

Kofi couldn't believe it. How could he have been on Clipper FM last Saturday and now the whole thing was shut down one week later? It didn't make any sense.

There was a sudden flurry of activity:

'What?'

'There anyone here?'

'What is this?'

'Where's Clipper, man?'

'Oi, Shanice, man, wha'gwan?'

And so on.

The chatter started to grow in volume and intensity. Gloria looked straight at Kofi (she was used to seeing him mess up, but it was usually just at home with Mum, Dad and Emmanuel). Kelvin looked straight at Kofi too (he was used to being with him when things went wrong, but it was usually at school). Shanice looked straight at Kofi (she had never seen him mess up like this before, and she didn't look impressed – at all).

Shanice opened her mouth to speak and Kofi instinctively winced, bracing himself for the yell. It was at this exact moment that a loud wail pierced through the air, and everyone stopped. Not even Shanice could scream *that* loud. But it wasn't her voice. It was a siren.

WEEUUW!

The siren blasted again, short and sharp. It was coming directly from below on the ground floor. Kofi leaned an elbow on to the balcony and craned his neck to peer over the edge. A small swarm of police officers were milling around two cars and a van, blue lights circling on top of each vehicle. Kofi felt his heart plummet into his shoes. It was the feds.

Ryu Spitter was the first to move.

'Come we go,' he said, hastily pushing through the now totally bewildered group.

'Go where?' said one of the Bs. 'We're on the top floor.'

It was true. There was quite literally nowhere to go. Everyone looked at Kofi. He started speaking before his brain had a chance to fully engage with his mouth.

'All we need to do is find a way into the flat, make our way through the secret entrance back down through the maintenance tunnels, escape into the disused car park, then we can lose the police and meet up again by the—'

'We should probably go down the stairs.'

Everyone turned to look at Kelvin, whose quiet interruption had stopped Kofi short.

'Uh, yeah ...' said Kofi. 'Or we could do that.'

*

The procession of kids filed their way down the eight flights of stairs back to the ground floor. No one spoke. They hadn't done anything wrong but they all knew that they had just been about to. It was impossible to pretend that jumping on air on a pirate radio station was a good idea, or that you didn't know that a pirate station was illegal.

'I'm running ...' whispered Barz Kid as they approached the main entrance past the disused lift.

'No you ain't,' hissed Gloria. 'If you run, the police

143

will just get annoyed, and we'll ALL be in more trouble than we are now. So stay put, and shut up.'

Kofi was almost surprised that Barz Kid didn't respond with a *Yes, miss* the way Gloria had put him in his place. She could be frighteningly like Mum when she wanted to. And she was right.

The sun was dipping fast in a cloudy sky as the group shuffled sheepishly out of the entrance. They were surrounded. Kofi scanned the faces of the assorted police officers, looking away quickly whenever any of them came close to making eye contact. He couldn't help but notice that they were all white. That was the way it always seemed to go: teachers, politicians, police – almost anyone who had any authority seemed to always be white, apart from Mum and Dad of course. And aside from the Portuguese family, the Italian family and the few Irish families on the estate, almost everyone who lived where Kofi lived was black. That was just the way things were.

'Over there.' The policeman spoke with a gruff impatience and pointed a thick finger towards the nearest wall.

'But what have we even done though?' one of the group protested.

'We're asking the questions here,' snapped another

officer. Kofi could hear a note of irritation in his voice, with a growl a bit like Mr Redge at school whenever Kofi got sent to the head teacher's office. '*Line up.*'

Kofi swallowed and his throat felt dry. It was taking all of his willpower to not just run away, but Gloria was right – doing that would only make things worse. He stole a glance at Kelvin, whose eyes were wide enough to show the whites all round. He looked terrified. Shanice's face was impossible to read, but he noticed she was picking frantically at her nails with the same fingers of one hand and seemed to be struggling to breathe normally. Everyone else was in various stages of shock or enforced silence. It was tense, and they were feeling nervous.

'I said, *line up.*'

The voice wasn't angry, but it was firm – and loud.

The kids started shuffling towards the wall with a few muffled complaints.

A youngish-looking officer stepped forward while Kofi turned, his back making contact with the dusty brick. He had brown eyes and a spattering of freckles across his cheeks. When he spoke, his voice was soft and low.

'We're just needing to, to ask you a few questions,' he said, almost in a whisper. It sounded to Kofi like he was making an apology – totally different to the other police officers who had spoken so far.

'Yeah,' rasped the growler. 'There's been a bit of trouble round here and you lot ...'

He paused to look each of them in the eye.

'And you lot shouldn't *be* here.'

Kofi saw Freckles's gaze darting from left to right.

Then he saw Shanice look up sharply.

'But what have we done though?'

It sounded more like a statement than a question. Even the growler was momentarily taken aback by how abruptly she had spoken. Gloria opened her mouth and raised a hand to warn Shanice to stop, but Shanice was indignant. The last time Kofi had seen her look like this, she had been just about to slap him on the back of his head.

'What have we done?'

Shanice put her arms out as if to say '*Well?*' and looked up and down the line of MCs. Kofi stole a quick glance at Kelvin, whose eyes were somehow even wider than before. He could feel the energy shift.

'You lot are *racist,* man.'

Shanice pointed at the growler square in the face, making him flinch slightly. Ryu Spitter gasped audibly. You did not get up in a fed's face like that.

A female officer stepped forward promptly but the

growler put out a thick arm to block her progress. His neck was starting to get red at the base of his collar.

'*What* did you say?' he muttered threateningly. But Shanice was undeterred.

'I *saai-id* . . .' She rocked her head from side to side as she broke the word down into two syllables. 'I *saai-id* that you lot are racist. Cha!'

You could almost hear the word *stupid* tagged on to the end of her sentence. She was clearly thinking it in her head. Kofi covered his mouth with his hand while a few of the MCs tried to muffle a giggle. The female officer raised both hands in an attempt to calm things down, but if the growler wasn't angry before, he definitely was now.

He inched closer to Shanice, grimacing at her. She didn't even blink.

'You'd better watch your tone, girl,' he hissed through gritted teeth. Her reply was instant.

'Or what, *bruv*?'

There was another audible intake of breath. Did she just call a policeman *bruv*? The unmistakable threat of a clash rippled through the air. Kofi found himself shivering and it had nothing to do with the cold. Shanice had lost it. She was shaking and looked as though she might cry. Or worse.

'I said OR WHAT, BRUV.' Her words came out in a shout, with a slight warble and voice crack at the end. Kofi felt his stomach flip in a dreadful lurch as he realised that everything that was happening was his fault. If he hadn't broken Dad's camcorder he would never have needed the money from subs, meaning that he would never have led everyone here and roped Shanice into his crazy plan. She wouldn't be here now about to get thrown into the back of that van over there. Because that's what was going to happen – he was certain of it.

Kofi closed his eyes.

'Hey!'

'Be quiet ...'

Shanice's and the growler's voices overlapped each other as Kofi opened his eyes to see what had just happened. He was met with the sight of Shanice's wrist being expertly gripped by the police officer. He held it at an awkward angle, making Shanice go dumb with shock. Freckles had one hand on the little radio on his lapel and a few other officers had taken a step forward. A few of the MCs, led by Ryu Spitter, had instinctively lurched forward, various combinations of fear and anger on their faces. Kofi wanted suddenly to hold his big sister's hand.

'HEY!!'

The voice was shrill and loud and came from a direction far to the left of where the police were gathered. All eyes swivelled to see who it was. A figure was bustling their way towards the group, making a direct line for Shanice. Kofi saw that it was a woman, about his mum's age, wearing a pair of brightly coloured dungarees and an African-print headscarf piled high on her head. She spoke again, a thick East London accent rolling into the dusky air. Each word was thrown like individual and separate projectiles.

'Get your HANDS *off* of that girl!' she yelled.

Kofi's eyes searched the group to see if anyone had any idea who this head-wrapped saviour might be. He stopped when he got to Kelvin, whose eyes were locked on her face.

'M-Mum!' Kelvin gasped.

25

Kelvin's Mum to the Rescue

'M-Mum?' repeated Kofi in disbelief.

He looked closer at the figure, who was gaining on the now totally surprised police officer. It was indeed Kelvin's mum. Even though he and Kelvin were best friends, Kofi hadn't seen Kelvin's mum very often at all, so he didn't recognise her straight away. And regardless, he had never seen her look as angry as this. Her usually jovial appearance had totally transformed.

The policeman released his grip.

'How *dare* you put your hands on her!' shouted

Kelvin's mum, cradling Shanice out of the way with one arm. 'How *dare* you put your hands on any one of these kids!'

A round-bellied officer sighed deeply and took a few steps forward, extending a hand with the palm facing outwards as if to say *hang on*.

'Madam, please,' he began. 'We've had reports of groups of—'

Kelvin's mum put her palm in his face.

'I'm not interested!' she warned, drawing giggles from some of the rappers. 'I've lived on this estate for long enough to know when the police are harassing people for no reason.'

She was going for it now, her voice getting louder and her gestures becoming more and more theatrical.

'You're the po-lice! You're s'posed to be out here protecting people – not holding a bunch of kids up against the wall! It's like Swamp 81 all over again.'

Kofi leaned towards Kelvin with his hand against the side of his face. 'What's Swamp 81?' he whispered.

Kelvin whispered back out of the side of his mouth. 'A police operation in Brixton back in 1981 where h-h-hundreds of people were stopped and searched for ... for no reason. My m-m-m ... mum talks about it all the time.'

Kofi looked at him and drew his chin into his neck. He'd never heard of it.

Kelvin's mum spun around to face PC Freckles, pointing directly into his face.

'You gonna arrest 'em? You have any suspicions about them?'

He faltered, stumbling for a response.

'Didn't think so,' she continued with a fold of her arms. 'It's cos *they ain't done nothing wrong, love.* They're *kids*! And if they have done something wrong, you go through their parents first.'

She jabbed her own chest indignantly. 'Like *me*!'

'Rah,' said Little B to Barz Kid in mild wonder. 'Whose mum is this . . . ?'

'M-mine . . .' said Kelvin quietly. Even when she was saving the day he couldn't help but find his mum mortifyingly embarrassing. She was powering ahead.

'Oh, I know the law, believe you me – and unless you have a reason to arrest *any* of these kids *right now*, I suggest you get back into your little cars and get out of this estate before I *give* you a reason to arrest me!'

There was a sharp intake of breath accompanied by a few *oooohs*, as if Kelvin's mum had just delivered some devastating bars in a clash. Which, to be fair, she kind of had. A female officer coughed lightly, clearing her throat.

'Madam, I think—'

'Don't you *madam* me,' Kelvin's mum interrupted. She was incensed. 'You got any kids? You want them in handcuffs, do you? You happy for *PC Plod* over there to break their arms?'

The officer didn't get a chance to answer.

'Go on, clear off. Or you'll be hearing from my lawyer!'

The police started shuffling back to their cars, a few of them muttering into their radios. It was clear who had won. Kelvin tapped his mum lightly on the shoulder.

'We don't have a lawyer,' he whispered.

'I know,' she whispered back with a mischievous gleam in her eye. 'But I've *always* wanted to say that.'

In a few moments, the convoy of police vehicles was making its way out of the estate, lights flashing but sirens silent. Ryu Spitter started to lead a low cheer, waving the police on their way. The sense of relief was palpable. Kofi felt his chest physically sag as he exhaled a long, deep breath. Like everyone else, he had been shaken up by the whole ordeal and joined in with a few rounds of *phew* and *that was close* and *you all right?* and *I can't believe it.*

'Come on,' said Kelvin's mum, hitching her handbag higher up on her shoulder. 'Let's go.'

Kelvin gave a sheepish half-wave to the assembled crowd, and a few of the MCs started spudding fists and making their exits. Shanice stepped forward.

'Thank you,' she said simply.

Kelvin's mum smiled. 'Not a problem, my love. C'mere.'

She extended her arms in a wide invitation, head leaning to one side, chin drawn back into her neck. Shanice looked like a puppy as she leaned in for the big hug.

The sudden appearance of Leroy at Kofi's shoulder made him jump slightly.

'Leroy!' gasped Kofi, putting one hand on his chest and the other against the wall.

'Sorry I'm late, man,' said Leroy through a mouthful of crisps. 'What'd I miss?'

26

Sorry, Emmanuel ...

'You did *what*?' cried Emmanuel in disbelief.

He fell into the sofa, touching the sides of his head with the fingers of both hands.

'I'm gonna have to tell Mum and Dad,' he said, blinking.

Kofi kicked Gloria in the leg.

'Ow!' she said, thumping him in the arm.

'I told you we should have lied!' Kofi hissed, rubbing his arm.

'No!' exclaimed Emmanuel, standing up. He started

pacing around the small front room in long, aimless strides. 'Less lying, Kofi, *less* lying!'

Kofi opened his mouth to speak but Emmanuel cut him short.

'I can't believe you two went to a pirate radio station – they're *illegal*.'

Gloria shifted her weight on to one hip and let her hand fall back at the wrist. 'Well, actually, I haven't *technically* even been on the pirate radio station, so . . .'

Emmanuel gave her a withering look. 'Gloria, you should know better,' he said in a serious voice. 'Kofi's the one that gets in trouble.'

Kofi decided to fight his own corner. 'You listen to pirate stations all the time!' he blurted.

'That's – that's different!' Emmanuel replied unconvincingly. 'The police don't come around here just to mess about. You could have been arrested.'

'We didn't even do anything!' said Kofi.

'That's not the point!' said Emmanuel, making another route around the front room back to the sofa. Kofi looked at his sister in a silent plea for help, but she was looking at her shoes. He could tell that she knew they were in the wrong, and when Mum and Dad found out, they wouldn't see the situation any differently.

That's when Kofi's mouth started moving – without allowing his brain the chance to give the all-clear.

'We didn't have a choice, man! We needed the rappers to go on the radio to get the money to pay for Dad's cam—' He stopped and put a hand over his mouth, turning to look at Gloria with wide eyes.

'Don't look at me ...' said Gloria with one raised eyebrow.

Emmanuel made a face like he was trying to work out a complicated sum without a calculator. 'Dad's cam ... *corder*?'

He stopped completely.

'Wait, what have you done with Dad's ...'

Interrupting himself, Emmanuel dashed out of the front room to the storage cupboard in the hall. Kofi and Gloria looked at each other as they listened to the sounds of his frantic opening and rummaging. Kofi winced as the seconds ticked on.

When Emmanuel reappeared at the front room door, he was holding a bag of flour in one hand and an empty camcorder box in the other. He was aghast.

'FLOUR, Kofi? *FLOUR?*'

Kofi's arms fell limp at his sides. The decoy didn't really work if someone actually went as far as opening the box. Gloria couldn't help herself, bursting out into a snort of laughter.

'Sorry, Kof,' she said, flopping on to the sofa and wiping her eyes with the back of her hand. 'Anyway, look on the bright side. At least I can't blackmail you any more.'

27

Caught!

If you wanna make a splash then
you should live in the sea
If you wanna see a rapper you should listen to me
Cos I got a little buzz – coming like I'm a bee
And I'm doing it so easy like it's nothing to me
This is nothing to me – but it's something to you
And they call me Young L, blud, how do you do?
You don't wanna mess with me and
you can't test with the crew
I'm about to school a rapper it's a lesson for you

Leroy stood with a crumpled sheet of A4 paper in his hand, slightly out of breath, looking down at Kofi expectantly. It was lunchtime in the library, and he had just finished delivering some new bars that he had written, testing them out on his friend.

'Well?' he said hopefully.

Kofi had his head turned, gazing across the library through the glass panel that led to the main corridor. He was miles away.

'Kofi!' Leroy picked up a stubby pencil and threw it at Kofi, hitting him in the chest.

'Hey, ow!' Kofi reacted, snapping out of his daydream and turning to scowl at Leroy.

Leroy sat down at the table, leaning his arms on the back of the chair, which was turned backwards.

'What's wrong with you, man?' probed Leroy, a tone of annoyance in his voice. 'You still worrying about yesterday?'

Kofi gave him a withering look. He momentarily felt his face make the exact same expression he'd often seen his sister make. And, come to think of it, his mum too.

'We almost got *arrested*,' said Kofi, poking at the pencil on the tabletop. Leroy laughed big and loud.

'*And?*' he said with a grin. 'Didn't you and Kelvin break into the big library on the high street last year?

And didn't you run a *Street Fighter* tournament with fake coins? Now you're acting like you don't like getting in trouble all of a sudden?'

Kofi leaned back on two legs of his chair. He had to admit, Leroy was kind of right. Kofi was no stranger to getting into trouble, even after only one year in secondary school.

'Technically, we broke *out* of the library,' he said finally, while Leroy rolled his eyes. 'Anyway, that was different.'

What Kofi didn't add was how worried he was about being in the biggest trouble of his life ever, once Mum and Dad realised what he'd done to Dad's camcorder. Emmanuel had given Kofi one day to own up and explain, otherwise he would tell them himself. Kofi hated when people made him take responsibility like that. He would much rather just ignore the problem and hope that it went away by itself. But at twelve years old, he was starting to appreciate that life didn't always work out like that.

Looking left to right, Leroy reached into his inside blazer pocket and pulled out a full, warm hamburger that he had picked up from the canteen. He took a big bite, speaking through chews.

'What you worried for, man?' he chewed. 'It's a

minor. Listen, I get stopped by the feds all the time.' Chew chew chew. 'They just ask your name and how old you are, you give a fake name and say ten, and they leave you alone, innit.'

Kofi looked at him dubiously. He wasn't so sure. For all his antics and last year's adventures, he hadn't got anywhere near the point of being comfortable with being stopped by the police, and he never would. Years of being told by his parents not to hang out on the estate all the time had given him a healthy fear of getting into trouble with the law. Mum and Dad had always worried about the police harassing groups of kids, and their solution was to avoid being in those groups in the first place. School was different – that was just teachers. But with the police, you could end up in prison.

'It was scary, man,' he explained to Leroy, a pained expression on his face. 'If it wasn't for Kelvin's mum, we would have ended up in that van, I swear.'

Leroy did another quick sweep and pulled a whole bottle of fizzy orange out of his other inside pocket. Kofi vaguely wondered what else he had in there.

'Where is Kelvin anyway?' asked Leroy after a swig of his drink.

'Don't know,' replied Kofi, peering out towards the corridor. 'Haven't seen him since first break . . .'

At that point, a large figure appeared from around a nearby display of books, heading straight for the two boys. It was Mr Rufferty, head of Design Technology and one of Redge's deputies. He was a tall, round man who always wore a white coat and a full tool belt. It gave him a slightly menacing look and even though he was big, the kids at St Campions somehow knew better than to ever cuss him for it – even out of earshot. You got the vague impression that he knew how to protect himself.

'*Simpson. Mensah.*'

Rufferty had a habit of only ever addressing students at the school by their surnames. Back in Year 7, Kofi had got a discipline mark for saying 'Call me Kofi' in the very first technology lesson of the year.

Leroy hastily stuffed his drink back into his armpit and tried to look like he wasn't eating in the library. Rufferty arrived at their table with a furrowed brow, his tool belt clanking quietly with each step. The boys were tucked away in the furthest corner of the library.

'Mrs Wagg said you were in here. Come on. Mr Redge wants you both in the office.' He paused for effect. '*Now.*'

'The office?' asked Leroy, incredulous. He licked his fingers. 'What did we do? Mrs Wagg lets us come in here, man, just ask her.'

Rufferty looked at him with a face that was as uninterested as it was irritated.

'Come on,' he sighed. 'Follow me.'

He made to leave and Leroy looked at Kofi, confused. Kofi shrugged and put his hands out, palms up. He was confused too. Leroy stood up.

'If this is about yesterday, I wasn't even there,' said Leroy defiantly.

Kofi's heart sank. 'Yeah, but I *was*,' he said in a panic. 'What's Redge gonna do?'

28

Redge's Office

Kofi's mind was racing as fast as his heart was beating as he walked alongside Leroy, behind Rufferty, on the way to Redge's office. The corridors were busy with students heading to and from the canteen. What was going to happen? What did Redge want from them? What if he had found out about yesterday? Kofi was fast realising he didn't have any of the answers.

Leroy maintained his usual casual bop, sneaking another bite of his burger as they turned a corner.

'Stop eating food out of your pockets,' hissed Kofi. 'How much trouble do you want us to get in?'

Leroy grinned through a mouthful of burger. Kofi seriously started to wonder if he had any fear at all.

They arrived at the little foyer outside Redge's office. It was a part of the school that most students never saw, unless they found themselves in trouble with Redge himself, so naturally Kofi had been there more than a few times.

'Simpson – sit here,' instructed Rufferty with a faint clank of tools. He was pointing at one of four chairs lined up next to each other. Leroy sighed theatrically and fell into one of them, spreading his arms wide across the backs of the chairs on either side.

'How long's this gonna take?' he asked casually, inspecting his fingernails.

For a split second, Rufferty's face looked like someone had just told him he didn't know his own birthday. Then he decided against reacting to Leroy and knocked twice sharply, before twisting the doorknob and pushing the door open.

'Mensah – you first. *In.*'

Kofi didn't have much of a choice. In he went.

The scene he was greeted with took him by surprise. As expected, Mr Redge was sitting at his desk, looking sweaty and annoyed as usual. But unlike usual, there was a guest sitting on a high-backed chair in the corner. The guest looked up and his eyes met Kofi's. Kofi recognised him instantly.

'Clapman!' exclaimed Kofi, unable to hide his surprise.

'Who?' growled Redge. He was already in a bad mood.

Kofi started to stammer a response. 'We usually— It's what— He's from the – he claps at us when . . .'

All eyes were on Kofi, wondering what on earth he was trying to explain. Kofi clapped feebly, feeling the energy drain out of his explanation.

'Never mind,' he finished quietly.

Redge leaned forward at his desk.

'I'm a busy man,' he began, not even trying to hide his disdain. 'A very busy man.'

He stood up and locked eyes with Kofi, leaning his full weight on the desk with both hands.

'A very, *very* busy man.'

Kofi wondered why he was taking so long.

Redge suddenly pointed at him with a stubby pink finger, making Kofi jump. It was as if he could read minds.

'But I'm not too busy for this!' His voice rumbled like a bus with too many people on board.

'When students from *my* school are caught making *public* disturbances, in *school uniform* –' he paused to crick his neck and the rest of the sentence was said darkly – 'I take that *personally*.'

Kofi's eyes widened in alarm. He was more scared now than when the police were chasing him through the estate. Redge turned to Clapman.

'This him?' he asked, pointing at Kofi without looking at him. Clapman turned his attention to Kofi, who was now almost completely bewildered. He hadn't been to Clapman's two-at-a-time shop since . . .

Then it dawned on him. His head rocked backwards and he closed his eyes, suddenly realising what this was all about.

Clapman looked from Redge to Kofi and nodded gravely.

'Yep,' he said, still nodding. Kofi's blood ran cold. Clapman continued. 'He's one of them, but he's not the one who took the money.'

Money?

Kofi's head tilted 45 degrees. 'What money?' he blurted out.

'Don't play dumb with me, Mensah,' rasped the head teacher, striding out from behind his desk. 'The money one of *you* lot stole from this gentleman's shop!'

Kofi's mind was tripping over itself trying to make sense of all this new information.

'You know what happened in that shop, because you were *there*,' he muttered menacingly, looking down at Kofi from barely a metre away. 'And one of you raided the till while it happened. Took a wad of cash, didn't you. *Didn't you?*'

Kofi was mortified.

'I – I . . .'

He couldn't get any words out.

'You sure it wasn't him?' pressed Redge, turning to face Clapman again. Kofi could see how much Redge wanted him to get in trouble for this.

Clapman shook his head.

'Nah, boss,' he said flatly, and Kofi very nearly put his palms together in a silent prayer of thanks. 'Not him. It was the other one, the loud one. About this big.'

Clapman raised a hand to somewhere just above Kofi's height.

Redge looked so disappointed that Kofi almost started to feel sorry for him. And then the obvious question flew into his mind: *Who took the money then?*

'Get the next one in here,' barked Redge, returning to his desk with angry little steps while flapping his hand towards the door. 'And get him out of here.'

Kofi didn't need a second invitation to leave. He spun on his heel and made straight for the door, wrenching it open from the handle before Rufferty had a chance to get there himself. The door swung open, revealing Leroy, sitting as they had left him, only looking more bored than ever. Kelvin looked down at his black Nike Airs and vaguely wandered if it could have been him that stole the money. Leroy was a rudeboy, no doubt, but would he actually steal money from a shop? That seemed way too extreme, even for him.

Before either boy had a chance to acknowledge the other, let alone speak, Rufferty had summoned Leroy to his feet and beckoned him into the office.

'*You*,' instructed Rufferty to Kofi with his typical trademark directness. 'Get yourself to class.'

Then the door closed before Kofi could respond.

The bell rang for the start of period five. Kofi thrust his hands into his trouser pockets and started making his way to the lesson. It was English with Mr Downfield. Usually that meant . . .

'GET OFF ME, MAN.'

Kofi whirled on his feet to see what the sudden commotion was, and what he saw made him cover his mouth in shock.

Leroy was flying out of Redge's office, his face in

a deep, deep scowl, arms flailing in the universally accepted signal for *Don't touch me*. Rufferty was close behind, but failing completely to control the boy. Redge was standing in the door with a look of demonic glee on his red, sweaty face. He didn't like Leroy just like he didn't like Kofi, so cornering him for the crime was looking like a Good Day. Clapman was on his feet too, watching the scene unfold.

'*That's* the one – that's the loud one I was talking about!'

No way, thought Kofi. He must have said it was Leroy who stole the money!

'Leroy?' called Kofi, but it was like Leroy couldn't hear him. He was at that point in his anger where no one could bring him down, shrugging off teachers with no care for how much more trouble he would get into. With a wild swing of the shoulder, he threw Mr Redge off balance, who stumbled backwards, scraping into a chair. Time paused as Redge scrabbled to keep his footing.

Kofi gasped.

You did NOT shove a teacher. Especially Mr Redge. If Leroy wasn't in trouble before, he was in a whole world of trouble now.

Then, just as quickly as he had appeared, he was

gone, around the corner and back into the main school, with Rufferty trotting behind, calling his name and trying to get him to stop. Kofi was glued to one spot.

The late bell rang, signalling period five. Redge had regained his balance and was patting his shirt front in mild shock. He'd just been pushed by one of his own students.

'*Class!*' he shouted at Kofi.

Kofi nodded twice and paced off at speed towards English.

'Walk!' he heard Redge shout behind him, making him slow his steps right down for fear of another mad encounter. But his heart, he noticed, was beating faster than ever.

29

The Cassette Tape

All the way home, Kofi couldn't shake the feeling that something wasn't quite right. Leroy was no angel, that's for sure, but Kofi couldn't believe that he would steal money from a shop.

For the first time in a while, he headed straight for home, lost in his thoughts about what had happened that afternoon. He was turning the whole situation over in his head, this way and that, trying to figure it all out – and getting nowhere. There was already a small crowd of kids at the minicab office playing *Street*

Fighter II on the arcade machines. Someone turned and spotted Kofi walking. It was Little B, one of the rappers who had paid subs to go on Clipper FM. After what had happened at the estate, Shanice and Kofi had already given all the MCs their subs money back. Little B tapped a friend on the arm before striding out to meet Kofi.

'Yo,' he asked, with genuine concern, 'what happened to Leroy, man? Is it true he punched Rufferty and got kicked out of school?'

School rumours grew like balloons.

'Dunno.' Kofi shrugged. 'Does that sound like something he would do?'

The two boys looked at each other as if to say *maybe*. The sound of a bus chugged into the scene and Kofi turned to check if it was his. It was the 16A.

'That's my bus, man,' he said, spudding fists with Little B. 'I'm out.' And he jogged towards the stop.

Sitting on the top deck, Kofi gazed out of the window, wondering what would happen to Leroy now. As the bus wound its way towards the estate, he spied the alleyway entrance to the car park cyphers down at street level. Even though it had only been a couple of weeks, the rapping, the excitement, the videos . . . it all seemed like a million years ago now.

The estate was quiet. The absence of the pirate radio bass, now that Kofi knew that the station was over, made the silence feel louder than ever, reminding Kofi of everything that had gone wrong. He almost didn't notice T, Patrick and Edward hanging in one of the first-floor walkways, Edward with a lollipop in his mouth and Patrick squinting away without his glasses on. T shouted down to get Kofi's attention.

'*Yo,*' he called.

'Sup,' replied Kofi. He was still processing his thoughts, but it was good to see a familiar face, especially with Kelvin absent from school that day.

'I heard the feds almost put you in a van,' T stated matter-of-factly. He shook his head. 'You need to learn when to *run,* Kof.'

Kofi nodded. T continued.

'Can't believe the radio station got raided, man ...' He spoke in a slow lament, like an old man who had seen it all go wrong a thousand times before. 'They never let us have nothing...'

Kofi was starting to see what he meant. With a sudden lurch in his stomach he remembered how much trouble he was going to be in over the camcorder, replaying the moment it had fallen from the balcony on the top floor. He winced, and it was as if T could read his mind.

'No new camera then?'

'Nope ...' said Kofi helplessly. 'I need to get home. Catch you later?'

T laughed. 'Rudeboy, catch you *never*. Your mum ain't *never* letting you out again and you know it.'

Kofi had to admit, T was probably right. He nodded a quick farewell, shouldered his rucksack higher on his back and set off on the walk of doom back to the flat.

Soon enough, Kofi was up on the fifth floor, letting himself in through the front door. He could hear the sound of the TV coming from the front room. It was Gloria. She was sprawled on the three-seater, still in her uniform, sipping Ribena and munching on toast.

'What are you doing here?' said Gloria, craning her neck to see her brother coming into the living room.

'I live here,' replied Kofi, dumping his bag and reaching for a slice of toast. Gloria slapped his hand away.

'Ouch!' said Kofi, pouting. 'That hurt!'

She ignored his complaint. 'So, you ready to fess up?' She turned with mock concern in her eyes. 'Dad's going to be so unhappy when he finds out what you did.'

Kofi crumpled into the single-seater, looking so defeated that his sister almost felt bad for him.

'Don't worry,' she said sympathetically. 'I heard that Ghanaian boarding schools are really nice this time of year.'

Laughing at her own joke, she scooped up the remote and continued.

'You won't even have to take a scarf,' she chuckled.

Kofi paused.

Scarf.

. . .

Scarf.

Kofi suddenly bolted upright in the chair and looked straight at his sister. She paused, holding the remote in mid-air.

'What . . . ?' she began. But Kofi wasn't listening. Springing to his feet, he darted out of the room and flew into the bedroom he shared with Emmanuel. He was looking for something.

Gloria was so intrigued by his sudden switch of mood that she followed him to the room.

'Kofi, you all right . . . ?' she asked hesitantly. It wasn't often that she saw her brother as focused as this. Whatever he had thought of, it was clearly important.

'Got it!' said Kofi triumphantly. He was brandishing

a camcorder cassette tape that he had retrieved from his collection, all jumbled up and stuffed in a plastic bag underneath the bunk bed.

'Got what?' asked Gloria, confused but intrigued. 'Kofi, what's going on? Kofi?'

But he had already flown out of the bedroom and returned to the front room, where he was busy putting the tape into a VHS adaptor, ready to play on the VHS recorder beneath the TV.

An image flickered into life on the TV screen. The point of view was from Kofi's perspective and the camera was pointed at Leroy, who was swaggering about and talking in a ridiculous American accent. They were on the street just outside the two-at-a-time newsagent's. Every now and again, Kelvin would pop into shot, looking nervous, before disappearing again. Kofi felt a surge of adrenaline as he realised that he *definitely* had the right tape. Gloria looked at her brother in disbelief.

'You stole Dad's camcorder to film *this*?'

'Shh,' replied Kofi, leaning forward intently, and Gloria clapped him on the back of the head. He rubbed where she had hit him but didn't flinch. Gloria couldn't help but lean forward too. The video was showing the boys entering the shop, just before everything got out of control.

'There!' declared Kofi, pointing at a smudge in the corner of the screen. He had paused the tape. Gloria was lost.

'What?' she said, trying to make out what he was getting so excited about.

'There!' repeated Kofi. 'That man, in the shop.'

Gloria leaned even closer. There, in the background, barely visible deep inside the two-at-a-time newsagent's, was an old man, shabbily dressed, wearing a red scarf.

'Hang on,' said Kofi, chewing his lower lip. He hit the fast-forward button and the images started racing ahead at twice the speed. Kofi's eyes flickered across the screen as the camera followed Leroy into the shop at double speed, spinning around to film a flood of St Campions blazers rushing in behind. Then it all became chaotic as the shelves were knocked into and Clapman attempted to get everyone out.

'You lot are terrible . . .' said Gloria quietly, shaking her head. 'See, this is why I don't tell people we're related.'

Kofi was barely listening.

'Look!' he exclaimed, pressing the 'pause' button. 'Red scarf! Look what he's doing!'

And sure enough, clear as day, the old man in the red scarf could be seen with one hand reaching into the till, his wrinkled fingers curled around a wad of notes. In all the confusion of the St Campions invasion, he had taken the opportunity to steal money from the till.

Kofi spun around to face his sister, eyes wide with indignation.

'Leroy's getting in trouble for stealing that money, but he didn't do it!' Kofi was animated, arms flailing as though he was trying to grab air. For now, all thoughts of the trouble that he was in had flown out of his mind. The injustice of what was happening to Leroy was bigger than all of that. Kofi felt a burning urge to do right by his friend, and now he had the evidence he needed to save the day.

Satisfied with the discovery, he pressed the 'eject' button with a look of determination on his face.

There was a whir, a click and a faint crunching sound.

Gloria and Kofi looked at each other, mirroring the horror in each other's faces.

Oh no.

Kofi pressed 'eject' again, a bead of sweat breaking out on his temple. He swallowed dryly.

Another crunch. Another whir.

The cassette wasn't coming out.

Kofi started to panic. Before his sister could stop

him, he'd reached his fingers into the slot where the cassette should have been.

'Kofi, no!'

But it was too late. Kofi was suddenly holding a cassette tape with half the insides spilling out into his open palms and the other half snarled up in the mouth of the machine. The tape was ruined, and there was no way of fixing it.

The front door clacked open, making Kofi jump.

'Kofi—?'

It was Emmanuel.

He came into the front room and stopped in his tracks when he saw Kofi crouched down by the telly.

'Hi, Emmanuel,' said Kofi hopefully. He held up the spools of brown tape. 'D'you know how to fix the video?'

30

Dad Speaks, Mum Speaks

'You did WHAT?'

Dad's eyes were wide all round as he stood staring at Kofi in disbelief.

It had been way harder than Kofi had thought, mustering up the courage to actually explain himself to his parents' faces. He'd begged Emmanuel to make something up instead, but his older brother had insisted that Kofi *take responsibility for his actions* and *do the right thing*. Kofi was very quickly discovering that this was easier said than done.

Mum was perched on the edge of the three-seater while Gloria and Emmanuel were in the kitchen. Kofi was standing in the middle of the front room with his arms behind his back, trying desperately to look cute and innocent. It wasn't working.

'So you're telling me we don't have my camcorder any more, because you took it to *school*, and broke it?' Dad looked more confused than angry. He paced forwards two steps and pointed at Kofi. 'What have I taught you about responsibility?'

Kofi blinked twice. 'Nothing?' he tried.

'No!' exclaimed Dad, exasperated. 'You are too old to be running around doing these irresponsible things all the time. I bought that camera for special occasions, and church.' He held up three fingers. 'When I was your age, I was working *three* jobs to help bring money home to put food on the table.'

Emmanuel and Gloria looked at each other. They were pretty sure the last time Dad had given this speech it was two jobs, for extra pocket money.

'Wasn't it two jobs, for more sweets?' asked Kofi innocently.

Gloria put a hand over her mouth to stifle a laugh and Emmanuel waved a hand to shush her. They weren't supposed to be listening.

Mum shifted her weight on the sofa. 'Kofi,' she said patiently, 'this isn't about the camera.'

Dad was taken aback. 'Yes it is!' he protested.

Mum continued regardless. 'It's about whether or not we can *trust* you, honey.'

Kofi looked down at his feet. Mum had a way of making him feel bad about things by being nice and telling the truth – at the same time.

'You can trust me, Mum,' he blurted out. 'I mean, I know I broke the camera but when the police—'

He stopped mid-sentence, realising, too late, that he'd said too much. Mum's eyes narrowed.

'*Police?* What police?'

The air grew tense. Dad being annoyed was one thing, but when Mum got upset, it was serious. She stood up.

'Did you get in trouble with the *police?*'

Kofi knew that Mum's biggest concern was any of her kids getting into trouble by hanging out on the streets. The only time he had ever seen her get *really* angry was at the police station last year, when Uncle Delroy got arrested. It had taken her a long time to forgive her brother for putting Kofi in that kind of predicament.

'*Well?*'

Kofi began to stammer a response, but Mum pushed on.

'And you didn't tell me?' Traces of her Jamaican accent were starting to come through, which happened whenever she got upset about something. '*What* did I tell you about hanging out on the estate, Kofi?'

It was like she was telepathic. Kofi scrambled to work out what to say.

'It wasn't just me!' he exclaimed. 'I was with a few friends, and Gloria, when—'

'You were with *who*?' Mum didn't even turn to look in the direction of the kitchen. 'Gloria! Get in here – now.'

Gloria shuffled into the front room, shooting a look at Kofi that could have set off a fire alarm.

'What about my camcorder?' protested Dad.

'Not now, Samuel,' said Mum. Dad took the hint and sat down.

'*You two*,' said Mum, crossing her arms.

'Yes, Mum,' said the siblings sheepishly.

'Start *talking*.' Mum sat down gently, legs crossed, her face completely impenetrable. 'And mek it good.'

*

Later that night, Kofi was lying in his bottom bunk with his hands clasped behind his head. Emmanuel was on top and the flat was quiet. Both boys were wide awake. The faint sounds of life on the estate could be heard from outside: a few voices, a dog or two barking, and just beyond, the low hum of the main roads.

After accidentally revealing his run-in with the law, Kofi had been given a curfew, which basically meant that he wasn't allowed to be out any later than it took to come home from school. Gloria had been given a curfew too, which she wasn't too happy about.

'Mum's only doing it because she's worried about you, y'know,' said Emmanuel quietly.

'Easy for you to say,' Kofi replied. 'You get to stay out.'

There was a brief pause. The sound of a revving engine could be heard in the near distance.

'Emmanuel?' Kofi began. Even with everything going on, Kofi had other stuff on his mind.

'Mm?' his brother answered.

'If you knew someone was innocent ... but you couldn't prove it ... what would you do to help them?'

The top bunk creaked as Emmanuel shifted his weight.

'You're not innocent, Kofi,' he stated flatly.

'No, not *me*,' said Kofi. 'Someone from school. He's getting in trouble for something I know he didn't do.'

Emmanuel swung his head round the edge of his bunk to look Kofi in the eye. 'A friend of yours?'

Kofi nodded and grinned. 'Yeah. I know you don't have any, but friends are, like, people you want to help out and stuff.'

He just couldn't help being cheeky sometimes. Emmanuel sighed.

'Just be there for them,' he said finally. 'Don't worry about solving the problem – they need you for support. Talk to them. Listen. And remember, you need to be home straight after school, so there's no point getting caught up in stuff.'

Kofi thought carefully about what his brother was saying.

'Thanks, bro,' he whispered into the dark. 'Night night.'

Emmanuel reached a long arm out of the top bunk to switch off the light and the room was plunged into darkness. There was an ambient glow coming through the small window.

With his eyes wide open, Kofi lay in bed and decided to ... do the exact opposite of everything his sensible big brother had just said.

31

The Man in
the Red Scarf

'Kelvin, are you sure this is the place?'

Kofi blew into his hands and stamped his feet against the pavement, trying desperately to get warm in the cold afternoon air. Kelvin was standing next to him, wearing a thick jacket, woolly gloves, scarf and a hat with flaps that came down over his ears. He also had his satchel with him.

Kelvin nodded.

Kofi already knew that Kelvin would be sure, because Kelvin never forgot anything. He had remembered straight away that this was where they had first seen the old man in the red scarf, way back at the start of term. It was when they went to the pitches with the giant cool box.

The memory of that hot summer's day was making Kofi feel even colder. Kofi always left the flat in a hurry without thinking about what the weather was like, so he'd been caught in the cold without enough warm gear on. Kelvin was naturally the more sensible one, so of course he'd checked the weather forecast and wrapped up properly.

The two boys were standing on the high street opposite the bus stop. It was Saturday afternoon and Kofi had convinced Kelvin to 'play out', as everyone called it. They didn't have long: Kofi's curfew meant that he had to be home way before it got dark, and Kelvin had told his mum that he was just going to return a few books at the library. Since the incident with the police, both boys' parents had become reluctant to let them roam around too freely.

'H-How l-long have we been w-w-waiting for ...?' shivered Kofi, watching his breath rise into the air.

Kelvin reached into his satchel and pulled out a little flask of hot, milky tea. He popped off the lid and poured in the steaming brown liquid, before taking a few small sips and glancing at the digital watch on his wrist. Kofi looked at him with a combination of awe and wonder on his face.

'Who *are* you?' he said in disbelief.

Kelvin looked at Kofi over the top of his cup as he took another sip. 'Want some?'

Kofi was just about to gratefully accept the offer when something across the street caught his eye. It was a flash of red. And it was attached to an old man with a slow, shuffling gait.

'There!' He pointed suddenly, spilling tea on to the pavement. 'There he is!'

Before Kelvin had a chance to ask exactly what Kofi was planning to do, Kofi had begun marching across the street.

'Hey!' shouted Kofi over the hum of passing traffic. 'Hey, you!'

The old man looked up with a startled expression on his face. He looked left and right, then pointed at himself as if to ask, *Me?*

Kofi waited for a break in the traffic and jogged across to the other side of the road. He pointed at the old man with an indignant finger.

'*You* stole money from the shop and now *my* friend is getting in trouble for it!'

The old man jumped slightly, like he had just sat on something sharp. He pulled a plasticine face and hurried off down the high street.

'Hey!' repeated Kofi.

Kelvin had caught up with him after using the pedestrian crossing further along. He sidled up next to Kofi, cup of tea in hand.

'He's getting away!' said Kofi. 'Come on.' And with that, he set off at a trot after his target, with Kelvin following close behind.

Kofi was angry. Never before had he felt the sting of injustice like this. Leroy had been suspended and would most likely be expelled, and Kofi had seen evidence that he had done nothing wrong. Now the real culprit was trying to run away from owning up. It wasn't fair.

The two boys were moving at a brisk walk, cutting through pedestrians on the busy pavement. The old man was not far ahead. He was walking like one of those funny speed walkers in the Olympics, all elbows and wiggling hips, glancing behind himself every few steps to see if the boys were catching up.

'Um ... so ... are we chasing him then?' asked Kelvin, putting his flask back into his satchel.

The old man turned his head.

'Stop ... chasing ... me!' he called out in a thin voice.

'I'll take that as a yes,' said Kelvin.

They sidestepped nimbly through a group of shoppers outside the entrance to the market. The old man was walking even faster now, looking over his shoulder with increasingly nervous twitches. He was panicked. Then he momentarily disappeared from view as a crowd of passengers poured off a bus that had arrived at a bus stop.

Kofi looked left and right, briefly lost as to where the old man had gone. Kelvin suddenly pointed. 'That way,' he said.

The flash of red had just disappeared around a corner further up the street. The boys took off at a jog to catch up.

'OK, here's the plan, when we catch up with him, I'll st—'

CRASH!

Kofi was on the ground surrounded by bags of spilled shopping before he'd even realised what had happened. He'd come around the corner too quickly and collided with an unfortunate old woman, who was now on the ground too, in a mild state of shock.

'Mrs Weaver!' exclaimed Kofi.

The old woman hoisted herself into a sitting position while Kofi and Kelvin scrambled to help her up.

'I'm so sorry, Mrs Weaver!' said Kofi, glancing in the direction of the escaping old man. 'I didn't see you.'

'That's OK, mi dear,' said Mrs Weaver through wheezes. She was being held at the elbow by Kelvin while Kofi hastily put her shopping back into the bags. Mrs Weaver had kind, twinkling eyes and spoke in heavy patois with a soft Jamaican accent.

'Wha'gwan wid all de rush?' she asked gently, fixing the knot that tied her headscarf.

Kofi looked desperately after the old man.

'Um, the library's closing…' he said distractedly. Kelvin patted his satchel. Mrs Weaver pursed her lips wisely.

'Well, jus remember: laang run, short catch, yuh hear mi?'

She spoke in old Jamaican proverbs that neither boy understood.

'Yes, Mrs Weaver,' they said in unison.

'And tell yuh mudda I said hello, yes?' she called after them as they dashed off.

'OK!' Kofi returned in a shout. But his attention was elsewhere. They reached a junction at the end of the street. There were four different roads the man in the scarf could have gone down. Kofi kissed his teeth, feeling momentarily Jamaican after his encounter with Mrs Weaver.

'Where'd he go, man?' Kofi asked helplessly.

And then:

'There!'

Kelvin's keen eyes had spotted the shuffling figure stepping on to a double-decker bus, just as the doors slid closed.

Kofi sprinted towards the bus but it was too late. He threw his hands up in defeat.

'Oh Jesus Chri—'

He stopped suddenly as a man and women carrying Bibles appeared out of nowhere. Kofi looked at them guiltily.

'Er, jeez Louise?' he tried.

They scowled at him in disapproval and walked off.

Kelvin had already run ahead and was at the spot where the old man had got on the bus. He stooped to the ground to pick something up. Then he returned to Kofi at a light jog.

'Look,' he breathed. 'He dropped this.'

Kofi examined the object in his friend's hand. It was an envelope.

'It's got an address on it,' continued Kelvin. 'And we know where that is.'

Kofi looked at Kelvin with wide eyes and furrowed eyebrows.

'Do we?' he said.

Kelvin leaned forward and ran his finger along the address.

'It's a flat,' he said. 'Next door to the pirate radio station.'

Kofi's eyes widened and his mouth fell open. The bus carrying the man in the red scarf had doubled back on itself and was now passing the boys on its journey up the high street. Through the windows on the top deck, Kofi could see the old man, standing, looking down at them. Kofi grinned and held the envelope up with two hands. The man's face fell and he started patting his sides and searching the inside pockets of his jacket. Kofi waved the envelope like a golden ticket and put his thumb against his nose, waggling his fingers.

'That's the express!' he said to Kelvin as the bus wound its way into the city. 'It doesn't stop at all until way over the bridge. I remember catching it by accident once and I ended up being almost two hours late for school.'

The bus disappeared around a corner. Kofi turned to Kelvin with a grin, flapping the envelope in front of his face.

'Kelvin,' he said with a sparkle in his eyes. '*We've* got somewhere to be.'

32

A New Discovery

It was getting dark. Kofi's mind was racing with ideas, and he was letting every last one of them pour out of his mouth as he strode along the busy high street. Kelvin was keeping pace by his side, listening carefully.

'OK, so if we know where he lives –' Kofi had his hands thrust deep in his pockets, a frown of concentration on his face as he walked – 'we can go to the police and tell them to go break his door down for the stolen money.'

'But we need evidence,' said Kelvin.

'Good point,' said Kofi, remembering the spools of brown videotape back at home. 'I doubt the feds would take our word for it.'

They reached a short crossing in the road.

'I've tried fixing the tape, but it's impossible,' said Kofi in frustration. 'Maybe if we—'

'Is that your brother?'

Kelvin was pointing at a tall figure across the street, looking vaguely in their direction.

Kofi jumped. 'Emmanuel!' he yelped, before ducking low to hide behind a newsstand. The metal flap banged clumsily as Kofi struggled to shrink himself into a tiny ball. Kelvin casually waved over at Emmanuel, who was now approaching.

'Are you mad,' hissed Kofi. 'Don't call him over!'

Kelvin shrugged. 'He's already seen us.'

Emmanuel hopped on to the pavement and kicked the newsstand lightly with the toe of his shoe. Kofi uncurled into a standing position and blinked theatrically at his brother.

'Oh, Emmanuel, wow, it's you!' he began. 'I was just coming back from the library with Kelvin and we were . . .'

He looked around helplessly.

'. . . playing hide-and-seek. You found me!'

Kelvin pulled a face.

'Kofi,' Emmanuel said with a slight strain in his voice. 'You're supposed to be at home. Mum and Dad put you on curfew, remember?'

'Oh, relax, man,' replied Kofi, dusting himself off. 'Anyway, listen, we found something out that—'

Emmanuel raised a hand to cut him off from explaining their recent big discovery.

'No. You're coming with me. I'm finishing up at work in fifteen minutes. I had to pop out to get some bin liners.' He shook a roll of black plastic bags. 'I can walk you home.'

Emmanuel looked at Kelvin and spoke in a much softer voice. 'Do you need me to drop you off at your block? On our way home?'

'Hey, why aren't you angry with *him*?' protested Kofi.

'Because I haven't broken my curfew,' replied Kelvin.

Kofi started to protest. 'But Manny, seriously, I've got—'

'Nope, come on,' Emmanuel interrupted. 'Let's go.'

As usual, Kelvin wasn't fazed. 'Thank you,' he said politely. 'But I'd better be going. My mum's expecting me.'

Emmanuel turned to look at Kofi, gesturing at Kelvin with one hand. 'See?' he said happily. 'Why can't you be more like Kelvin?'

Kofi mimicked his brother and stuck out his tongue. 'Man, you used to be cool,' he pouted.

'No I didn't,' Emmanuel replied, stepping into the road.

Kelvin hitched his satchel across his body. 'Well, to be continued, I guess,' he said.

'Yeah ...' replied Kofi, slightly deflated. 'See you at school. I'll work out what to do to get Leroy back.'

They spudded fists and Kelvin disappeared in the direction of home.

Across the road was the second-hand furniture shop that Emmanuel worked at on weekends and some evenings. It was a huge, double-fronted building with an ancient sign running in faded letters across the entrance. Everything in the shop was either old, dusty or broken. Emmanuel's job was mainly to move things out front and back again, or make room in the warehouse for new arrivals.

'I've just got to finish up for around ten minutes,' he said to Kofi as he ushered him into the main showroom. 'Wait in here and don't get into any trouble.'

His finger was pointing in Kofi's face. Kofi pulled it defiantly, making Emmanuel grimace.

'Why are you so childish sometimes,' he sighed.

'Because I'm a child?' replied Kofi.

Emmanuel pulled another face. 'Ten minutes,' he said, disappearing into another room. 'And please – don't touch anything.'

He made to leave, but then stopped and turned to face Kofi again.

'Kofi,' he sighed. 'That camcorder was really important to Dad. And you broke it.'

The powerful truth of Emmanuel's words made Kofi feel a sudden rush of guilt through his chest. There was something about the way his brother said it that made it hit home, hard. Kofi looked at the floor.

'You need to fix it,' continued Emmanuel.

Kofi looked up slowly. Emmanuel was right, and he knew it.

'Listen, stay here until I get back. We can work out how you're going to sort this all out later.'

And with that, he was gone.

Kofi was alone with the weight of his thoughts. His mind was usually racing with energy and ideas and this was the first time he'd stopped to let it all sink in. He knew he'd gone too far and he really didn't want to have let Dad down so badly. Again.

The back room was quiet. Piles of old furniture were scattered in a landscape of ancient wood, fabric and metal. Kofi started drifting aimlessly, tracing a finger along a dusty sideboard. He found himself wondering vaguely about all the people who had sat in these chairs and opened these drawers. It was like walking through the past.

That's when it caught his eye.

Over in the furthest corner from the door.

A table.

A large wooden table.

A large wooden table with a big brass handle on the front. And a deep, diagonal scratch, like a scar.

Kofi gasped.

Could it be?

He ran over and bent forward, arms open, checking to see if his memory was playing tricks on him.

It wasn't!

Kofi scanned the table for clues. He found a little white tag attached to one of the legs. 1-8-H-7-1, it read. Every item in the shop's back room had one of these tags. Kofi started searching through them, checking for matches. After a minute or so, he found what he was looking for. A wall cabinet, lying sideways on the floor, tagged with the same code as before: 1-8-H-7-1. Kofi snapped his fingers in celebration and bent to a crouch, opening the door. An empty tin clattered to the floor. Kofi scooped it up for inspection.

'Yorkshire Tea . . . !' said Kofi in wonder. 'I knew it!'

The table was from Linton's flat!

He pulled at the brass handle but it was stuck fast. He tried again, rattling it vigorously.

'Kofi!' he heard Emmanuel call from somewhere else. 'What are you doing in there!'

'N-nothing!' returned Kofi, giving the drawer one final rattle. His instincts were telling him to look inside. He was ready to give up all hope when he felt something give way in the turn of the handle. A slight click. With a careful half turn, the drawer scraped open, as if for the first time in years. He opened it fully. It was completely empty – apart from a small, yellowing rectangle stuck to the rough wood. Without thinking, Kofi reached in and peeled it away. It was an ancient photograph. Kofi squinted in concentration, scrutinising the unfamiliar image. Emmanuel's approaching voice made him quickly stuff it into his back pocket.

'Sorry I took a while.'

Emmanuel had appeared, jacket on, ready to go. Kofi sprang to his feet.

'We got a big delivery earlier and there was a bunch of electrical stuff that needed sorting,' he continued. 'Transmitters . . . speakers . . . cables . . . amplifiers . . . turntables too. Really cool gear actually.'

Kofi shook the cramp out of his legs.

'1-8-H-7-1?' he asked his big brother.

Emmanuel's face drew back in surprise. 'Yeah,' he said. 'How did you know that?'

33

No More Surprises

Kofi decided against telling his brother about the photograph. There hadn't been time to replace it, and he didn't really feel like getting into any more trouble than he was already in.

As they walked, Emmanuel explained how furniture often came into the shop from old flats and houses that were abandoned. That was what must have happened with 1-8-H-7-1. When the owners go missing, or die, or can't keep up with their rent, then the authorities step in and all the contents get taken in by the council.

It was all very interesting, but Kofi was only half listening, responding with half-hearted, distracted noises like *Mm* and *Uh-huh* and *Yeah*.

'You OK, Kofi?' asked Emmanuel as they entered the estate. Lights from windows created little yellow squares in the gloomy dark.

'Mm?' said Kofi, lost in his thoughts. 'Oh, uh-huh, yeah.'

Kofi had only seen the photograph that was now in his back pocket for a few brief moments, but he had fully committed the image to memory. There was a woman in a flowery dress and white gloves, standing next to a black man and a white man who were smiling at the camera and shaking hands. A thin, rectangular case was resting by their feet. The black man was wearing a smart suit and had a hat on his head at a jaunty angle.

Kofi looked up in the direction of the pirate radio station and wondered what secrets were held in that old, now silent, flat. Then he thought about Linton, who he hadn't seen – or heard – since going live on air.

At the door of the flat, five flights up, Emmanuel turned to face Kofi with his key in the lock.

'Listen,' he said, trying to sound stern. 'You got away with it this time, but no more surprises, OK? Mum and Dad don't need the stress.'

Kofi was half tempted to mimic Emmanuel again and be the annoying little brother, but he thought better of it.

'Yes, Emmanuel,' he said in an almost-drone.

Emmanuel nodded. 'Just remember,' he added with the final turn of the key, 'me bringing you home has saved you getting into trouble for breaking your curfew.'

Kofi's face was incredulous.

'You're welcome,' said Emmanuel, before adding. 'And remember: *no surprises*.'

But when he pushed open the door, Kofi was presented with a surprise so big that it made him physically stagger backwards, almost falling flat on his backside in the concrete walkway. His voice came out in a yell.

'*WHAT?!*'

34

Face-to-Face

'*You!*'

Kofi was pointing at the man who was standing in his hallway. The man was white, old, with more gums than teeth, and a red silk scarf around his neck. Yep, it was the man from the bus.

The old man was as surprised as Kofi was. He staggered slightly, instantly recognising this boy who, only minutes before, was taunting him from street level.

'What are you doing here?' they both said in alarmed unison. Then Kofi gathered his thoughts.

'I live here!' Kofi exclaimed.

'You *live* here?' replied the old man.

'That's what I just said!' snapped Kofi, too shocked to soften his tone. Emmanuel was perplexed.

'You two *know* each other?'

The old man said 'No' and Kofi said 'Yes', at the exact same time. At that moment, Mum appeared in the hallway.

'Boys, come in before all the heat gets out,' she began. 'This is Mr Thompson. He was helping Mrs Weaver up the stairs earlier and I invited them both in. She had bit of a fall today.'

Mrs Weaver? Kofi's mind rewound back to the moment he had clattered into her by accident when he and Kelvin had been chasing—

'Jim,' said the old man to Mum. 'Please, call me Jim. I'm a good friend of Mrs Weaver's. It was lucky I was around to help her get home.'

At that point, a shuffling Mrs Weaver also appeared in the now very crowded hallway. She looked straight at Kofi. He gulped. If she said anything about the collision, Kofi would be in massive trouble for sure. Biting his lip, he pleaded at her with his eyes not to tell anyone that it was him who had run into her earlier on. Somehow, miraculously, she seemed to get the hint, responding with an almost imperceptible nod of the head.

'Boys,' began Mrs Weaver slowly, 'your mudda is a good, good woman yuh na. I'm tekking over the cooking to say a likkle *thank you* for looking after me so.' She turned to look at Mum, who put up her hands in mock defence. 'And me nah tek no for an answer.'

Mum grinned. 'Come on, Mrs Weaver. You'll have to show me your secret recipe.' Then she addressed Emmanuel and Kofi. 'Mr Thompson is staying for dinner too. He's a good friend of Mrs Weaver's and helped her all the way home.'

Mr Thompson cut in with a simpering voice. 'I got on the express bus by accident, but the driver let me off before the bridge.'

Kofi shot an instant scowl at the old man, but he was too busy smiling and wringing his hands together in mock humility to respond.

'Dinner would be *lovely*,' he gushed at Mum. His eyes flickered towards Kofi in momentary panic. 'But, really, I have to – I have to go, so . . .'

Mum and Mrs Weaver started making a load of noises that collectively added up to Mr Thompson not going anywhere and staying to eat dinner whether he liked it or not. He briefly locked eyes with Kofi again, this time silently agreeing on a reluctant truce. For now. Mr Thompson bowed slightly.

'Thank you,' he grinned, flashing the pink gums. He was such an actor, Kofi thought.

As soon as Mum and Mrs Weaver had returned to the kitchen and Emmanuel was out of earshot, Kofi and the new house guest turned sharply to face each other.

'You little thief,' hissed Mr Thompson. 'Give me back my letter!'

Kofi retaliated with venom. 'Give back the money you stole!'

Mr Thompson crinkled his brow and laughed a hollow laugh. 'You can't prove anything!'

'Oh, can't I?' said Kofi, and stormed off in the direction of the kitchen. Mr Thompson was alarmed.

'No, wait!'

Kofi cleared his throat loudly and pointed with a straight arm. 'Mum, everyone, *that man* is a—'

But before Kofi could finish his announcement, Mrs Weaver had thrust a large, steaming dish into his unexpecting arms.

'Be a sweetie and tek dis to the table,' she instructed. 'It hot, so don' *rush*,' she added with a wink. Kofi suddenly found himself carrying the dish to the fold-up table.

'Gloria!' called Mum into the hallway. 'Dinner's ready – come off the phone now, please!'

The phone cord was stretched from the front room all the way to Gloria's box room. She'd been in there the whole time, probably, Kofi guessed, talking to Shanice.

'Co-ming, *Mum*!' bellowed Gloria from behind the closed door. Mr Thompson appeared in the front room doorway.

'That smells divine!' he gushed, and Kofi clenched his teeth.

*

Before long, Mum, Emmanuel, Gloria, Mrs Weaver, Mr Thompson and Kofi were all sat around the foldaway table, with the lamp casting its warm glow across the feast. It was excellent food: traditional Jamaican dishes cooked by the expert hands of Mrs Weaver, with some of Dad's leftover jollof rice and a few Ghanaian touches thrown in for good measure. Under normal circumstances, Kofi would be happily stuffing his face with rice, stew, plantain and spicy meats, but today he was too busy working out how to expose Mr Thompson. It didn't help that Mr Thompson seemed to be enjoying himself so much, praising every bite and filling the table with stories about the good old days, when Mrs Weaver had first arrived in Britain.

He had just finished telling a story about what the area looked like before the estates were built, when Gloria suddenly felt a swift kick in her leg from underneath the table.

'Ow!' She winced.

It was Kofi, trying to get her attention. She clearly hadn't recognised Mr Thompson from the video Kofi had shown her. Without a single word having to be exchanged, sibling telepathy kicked into gear.

I need to see you outside.

What for?

Just come, man!

Fine.

And she rose to her feet.

'Kof, could you help me find those extra serviettes you put somewhere,' she said smoothly. Kofi was still amazed at how naturally deceptive his sensible big sister could be when she needed.

Out in the corridor, Kofi spoke in hushed tones. 'That man is a thief!' he said hoarsely. 'He's the one from the video!'

Gloria momentarily drew a blank. Then she remembered. 'Are you sure?'

Kofi's shoulders sagged in exasperation. 'Yes, you idiot!'

Gloria's eyes went super-wide. 'Who you calling an idiot?' She kissed her teeth long and loud and swept back into the front room, grabbing a stack of serviettes along the way.

'No, wait!' tried Kofi, but it was too late.

Gloria sat back down in her seat and shot Kofi a look that was somewhere between disgust and the threat of physical violence. Mum was in the middle of listening to something that Mrs Weaver was saying in a low, whimsical-sounding voice. Kofi, now growing desperate, leaned in and beckoned Emmanuel over.

'Um, Emmanuel, could you come here for a sec, please? I need you to . . . reach something for me.'

Emmanuel looked up. He was momentarily confused. Kofi jerked his head backwards twice as if to say *Come on*. Emmanuel came, excusing himself from the table.

'Kofi,' he said in the corridor, perplexed. 'What's going on?'

'Mr Thompson is a *thief*,' hissed Kofi. 'That's what's going on!'

Emmanuel scratched his head. 'Mrs Weaver's friend, in there?' he said.

'*Yes*,' said Kofi. 'He's the one in the video.'

'What video?' said Emmanuel.

Kofi gritted his teeth and grunted in frustration. 'The one I broke the other day! Remember?'

Emmanuel's face was completely blank.

'Everything all right out there?' Mum's voice bounced into the corridor at a tone that both boys knew to be a warning more than a genuine enquiry.

'Coming, Mum!' they both said.

As they returned, Mr Thompson was rising to his feet, making the noises of a well-fed guest about to leave. Mrs Weaver was in the middle of offering to wash up, which Mum was refusing firmly.

'No, Mrs Weaver, you've done enough already. I didn't have all these kids for my guests to have to do their own washing-up, you know. Kofi will start on the plates now.'

She raised an eyebrow at her son. 'Won't he,' she said with authority.

'Yes, Mum,' said Kofi, flatly.

35

Emmanuel to the rescue

Minutes later, Mrs Weaver and Mr Thompson had left the flat and Kofi was elbow deep in a sink of washing-up. He was seething. Mr Thompson had stolen money from the shop and Leroy had taken the blame. And what's more, the radio station was shut down forever and all hopes of getting it back were sitting in a dusty warehouse on the high street. It was a disaster.

Emmanuel appeared with yet another stack of crockery in need of washing. Gloria was on the other side of the sink, drying.

'You all right, Kofi?' Emmanuel asked. Kofi didn't realise that he had been scrubbing the same plate for about two minutes straight.

'It's not *fair*,' he said with a scowl, chucking the plate into the murky water with a splash.

'It's only a bit of washing-up,' said Gloria. 'Grow up, bro.'

'No,' whined Kofi. '*Mr Thompson*. If only my video still worked.'

Emmanuel was wiping his hands on a tea towel.

'Oh, the one you broke? I remember now. I fixed it. It took a while, and I had to—'

Kofi didn't let his brother finish. 'Wait – you fixed it?'

He beamed and threw his wet arms around Emmanuel's chest in a soggy bear hug. 'I love you, Manny! I love you like a brother!' Wiping his hands on his trousers, he threw the sponge at Gloria and darted out of the kitchen.

Mum was reclining in the single-seater, chatting on the telephone while the television was on. Kofi marched up and snatched the handset from her, swiftly placing it back in its cradle.

Emmanuel and Gloria gasped.

Before Mum had a chance to fathom out what on

earth was happening, Kofi scooped up the newly fixed video cassette and pushed it into the open mouth of the VHS player. The TV screen flickered to life with the image of chaos in the two-at-a-time newsagent's. Kofi let it play for a couple of seconds, then hit 'pause' with a jabbing finger.

'*There*,' he said, emphatically, gesturing towards the screen like a magician doing the big reveal.

Clear as day, on the screen, was an old man in a red scarf with his whole hand in the till. It was definitely Mr Thompson. Kofi advanced the image forward by pressing 'play' and 'pause' a few times. In the video, one frame at a time, Mr Thompson could be seen removing a thick wad of notes.

Mum leaned forward to have a closer look, squinting with concentration.

'Mr Thompson is not who he says he is,' explained Kofi. 'He stole money from that shop and my friend is getting the blame for it. See?'

Mum stood up. Thoughts were clearly racing through her head, but no one quite knew what she was going to do.

'Get your coat,' she said.

36

Mr Thompson's Big Confession

Mum was walking faster than Kofi could keep up with, and he was having to trot beside her to stay in place. She was on a mission, striding through the gloomy concrete walkways and almost skipping down the shadowy stairwells.

On the ground floor, she looked left then right, then spotted her target in the dark. She set off without a word. Kofi jogged along after her.

'*Hey*,' she said forcefully as she neared him. Mr Thompson turned round and his face broke into a wide smile.

'Sonia!' he said warmly. 'What's up? Did I forget something?'

'Yeah,' snapped Mum. 'You forget to explain why you're stealing money from shops and letting little kids take the blame for it.' Her voice was iron.

There was a pause in the air as Mr Thompson's face fell. For a moment, he was aghast. Then his eyes dropped to the floor in shame. When he looked up, his face was completely ashen. Mum hadn't looked away the whole time. When she spoke, it was slow and certain.

'I think you'd better come back up,' she said, the faint traces of her Jamaican accent starting to poke through. 'Before I start making some calls you *really* don't want me to make.'

*

Back at the flat, Mum sat a fresh mug of tea in front of Mr Thompson and slid into the chair opposite him. He cradled the mug in both hands and murmured a weak 'Thank you', before taking a bleary-eyed sip. Kofi watched on silently. Mr Thompson looked defeated already.

They were seated at the foldaway table again, but this time, the atmosphere was completely different.

Mum and Mr Thompson were facing each other while Kofi was in a chair off to one side. Gloria was standing against the back wall with her arms folded while Emmanuel was leaning against the kitchen door frame. Dad was out at work. Mr Thompson looked around nervously.

'Would you mind if – if the children went away for this?' he stammered. 'I'd rather it was just you and me . . .'

Mum didn't flinch.

'Whatever you need to say to me, you can say to them,' she said. 'It was Kofi who found out in the first place.'

Yeah, thought Kofi, with a satisfied feeling in his chest.

Mr Thompson nodded and took a gulp of tea.

'OK,' he said. 'I'll start from the beginning.'

37

How It All Began

'I must have been about fifteen or sixteen,' began Mr Thompson. He had his hands clasped around his mug of tea.

'I'd never been any good at school, so I left the place as quick as I could. Hated it. All that sitting still listening to miserable teachers. When I got out, I had no qualifications or exams or anything. But I was too young to join the army, so I managed to avoid going to war. Lucky, I guess.

'One thing I'd always loved was music. Back in those

days, every pub in the country had a piano in it. Just a little upright one, nothing special. A lot of people even had them in their homes too. I taught myself to play at a friend's house, banging about on the keys when his mum wasn't around, but it came naturally to me. I've always been able to find a tune, and I can carry a bit of a tune myself. So I ended up going into pubs, working men's clubs, that sort of thing, just singing songs and tinkling the ivories for a few pennies at a time. I never thought that could be a way of making a living, but I started making OK money off it. A few bob a month – enough to get me own piano. In the pubs they'd call me little Jimmy T. "Here comes little Jimmy!" they'd say. "Give us a tune, Jim!" I loved it. Especially when they'd have a lock-in. We'd sing songs all through the night. It was glorious.'

As he spoke, Mr Thompson visibly started to relax, leaning back in his chair with only one of his elbows resting on the table.

'There was this one pub that I'd go to most weeks. Became my regular. Not too far from here actually – long gone now – just off the high street. It's a supermarket now … Anyway, I goes in one night and I couldn't believe what I was seeing. The place was full of coloured—'

He stopped short, suddenly alert, eyes darting around the room in a mild panic.

'Sorry,' he stumbled. 'I mean, um, black – black fellas. West Indians. We called them "coloured" back then. I mean, we—'

'It's OK,' interrupted Mum gently. 'Carry on.'

Mr Thompson cleared his throat and continued.

'You have to remember, there weren't many black people around at all back then. I'd actually never seen one up close until that night, but after the war, you'd see them all the time. When I got to the pub, I asked the landlord what was going on. He told me a load of West Indians had arrived just that night. They still had suitcases and everything. They were in great spirits too – happy to be in from the cold, I reckon. When I think about it now, the landlord must have been a really decent bloke. A lot of pubs wouldn't have even let them in.

'I pull up at the piano, all ready to play a tune, and this one fella – beautifully dressed – suit, hat, tidy moustache, everything, quietly asks if he could take the seat. I must admit, I had to ask him to repeat himself a couple of times. I was hopeless with the accent. But yeah, I thought, if the gaffer was OK with it, why not? A few of the local regulars were looking a bit sus about the whole thing and I think one or two might have even walked out. Terrible. So, this fella sits down, takes off his hat, puts his hands out like this—'

Mr Thompson put his hands out above an imaginary keyboard.

'And WHAM! He starts *playing*!'

Kofi jumped suddenly as Mr Thompson came alive in his memory.

'I'd never heard anything like it,' said Mr Thompson, leaning forward with a gleam in his eye. 'I thought the stuff I was playing in the lock-ins was fun, but this was something else. After that, I had to find out more. The piano player told me it was something called *calypso*, straight from Trinidad and Jamaica. I'd never heard of the places, but I was hooked. His mates were loving it – up dancing and all sorts. They really brought the sunshine into that pub. Fantastic.'

Kofi watched Mr Thompson reminiscing about that night all those years ago. His eyes were far, far away, gazing into nowhere.

'So anyways, I introduce myself and he tells me his name is Lloyd McLean. Pleased to meet you, I say, and we get talking. Turns out he's into music as much as I am. He's got one suitcase with him and he takes me to one side to show me what's inside. Halfway across the world from the West Indies to Britain and you know what Lloyd McLean is lugging around with him?'

Mr Thompson paused for dramatic effect.

'Records! Hundreds of 45s, all wrapped up and packed like precious jewels. I'd never seen so many, I'm telling you. It was like a treasure chest. I had to hear them. I was *desperate* to hear them. And that's when I had me an idea ...'

Mr Thompson grinned mischievously.

'I went straight up to the guvnor behind the bar and asked him if I could borrow his gramophone player instead of my usual payment for that week. I knew he had one upstairs you see, and for some mad reason, he said yes. Only thing was: we couldn't use it in the pub – licensing laws or something. So, me and Lloyd, we finish our drinks, round up his mates, and we carry that gramophone through the streets of London all the way to where they were staying. Can you imagine? Bloody heavy it was too. Good thing it wasn't raining.

'All the col— Sorry, I mean black arrivals ended up in a really shifty part of town. I didn't grow up rich or anything but even I didn't hang around there. And their rooms weren't very nice at all. But when we turned up with that gramophone ...'

The wistful, faraway look came back into Mr Thompson's eyes.

'. . . when we turned up with that gramophone and all them records . . . It was a hero's welcome. All these men and women, beautifully dressed, so welcoming, making a go of it . . . and me, little Jimmy the piano player. We put on record after record and had the best party I've ever been to. And I've been to some parties . . . We must have had fifty people in that place, from all over the tenement. There was even some rum from somewhere, and dancing too. My life changed that night.'

'What happened next?' whispered Gloria quietly. She was transfixed.

'I'll tell you,' continued Mr Thompson, smiling. 'Me and Lloyd became the best of friends. He would have liked to have got work as a musician, but ended up doing a bit of construction, odd jobs, that kind of thing. I was doing bits and pieces too, electrical work, things like that, so we stayed close. Meeting up over a song and a nip of rum became a bit of a weekly ritual. And I became a familiar face among all the other lot from Trinidad, Barbados, Jamaica. To be honest, if I'd had half the chance, I would have got on a boat or a plane myself and gone there. It sounded fantastic. I never managed it though. Never had the money.'

Mr Thompson's eyes flickered towards Kofi. Like his sister, Kofi was transfixed by Mr Thompson's tale.

'By the time you got into the 1950s, we were all getting older. Things weren't nearly as bad as during the war, but it was still tough. Work wasn't easy and money was hard to find. But Lloyd was a grafter, and he always told me that he wanted a family to provide for. You know what's coming next.'

Mr Thompson smiled warmly, teeth and gums.

38

Family Ties

'Her name was Gertrude. Lloyd knew he was going to marry her from the minute he first set eyes on her. He was that kind of chap – full of life and romance and big ideas. So I weren't surprised at all when he told me he was going to pop the question. Had a ring and everything. Must have cost him a fortune. Proper diamond on it. Real gentleman he was.

'It was around this time that all this started to get built.' Mr Thompson gestured widely with a sweeping arm. 'These tower blocks. It was a totally new idea – that you could live in the sky, on top of each other like this. I thought it was marvellous. Lloyd wasn't so sure. He always wanted a front door and a garden.'

He shrugged.

'Didn't matter to me. Besides, I've never exactly been lucky in love so I was alone too. One of these new "flats" sounded like the business to me.

'*February sixth, 1952,*' announced Mr Thompson proudly. 'That was the day I got the keys to my brand-new flat. I'll never forget the date. Same day that old Liz became the Queen. And now I had somewhere to put all my gear; all my music and electronic stuff. Lloyd was so happy for me, but he'd managed to get a house a bit further out. It was bombed during the war but he was going to fix it up and turn it into a palace to raise a family in. Would have done it too, I . . .'

Mr Thompson suddenly grew quiet. The mood shifted and a cloud seemed to hover over his brow. Kofi could tell something was wrong.

'What happened?' he asked simply.

Mr Thompson's eyes were foggy. 'Could I trouble you for another cup of tea?' he asked softly. Mum nodded, and looked over at Emmanuel, who wordlessly went into the kitchen and flicked the kettle on. For a few moments, no one spoke, letting the sounds of pouring water and a stirring spoon fill the air.

'Thank you,' said Mr Thompson gratefully, carefully taking the hot mug of tea from Emmanuel. He was ready to continue.

'We were walking home from the pub one night after work. It was raining, of course. Lloyd had just told me the news – that he and Gertrude were expecting. He was overjoyed. I was so happy for him and a bit jealous, mind, cos I knew my best friend wouldn't be able to come out so much any more. Childish of me when I think about it now. Haven't really thought about it in forty years ...

'There were four of them. Policemen. *Bobbies on the beat* we used to call them. They didn't like the look of Lloyd – said that he "fitted a description". Absolute nonsense of course. They were stopping him because he was black. They were happy to let me go; just wanted "a word" with Lloyd. Bloody racists.'

He took a sip of tea before carrying on.

'I wasn't having none of it. I told them coppers they was being racist. I'd had a few drinks so I was feeling brave. Stuck my beak right in. Got right in this one copper's face, I did. Lloyd was the sensible one. He tried to get me to leave it – said he'd talk to them. He was a peacemaker like that – always trying to calm things down. I should have done the same.

'I pushed one of them. Hard. He fell over. Then one of the other ones just went for me: got his truncheon out and swung it right for my face. That's when Lloyd stepped in. He didn't even think twice – put an arm out to block it. To protect me. He did that to protect *me*.'

Mr Thompson looked down at the table. When he looked up again, his eyes were red and misty.

'Two of them held me back while the other two grabbed Lloyd,' he said in a flat voice. 'By the time they'd finished with him, he could barely move.'

The tears rolled down Mr Thompson's cheeks. Kofi realised his eyes were stinging too. It was an awful story.

'He died later that week in the local hospital.' Mum made a small sound like a cough and a whimper. Mr Thompson's face was emotionless.

'The police said they acted in "self-defence". We were all devastated – his friends, his mates, all of us. But what could we do?' He searched in every face, looking so desperate and so lost that Kofi had to turn away.

'Life changed after that. I stopped seeing people, withdrew into myself. I just worked my little jobs and went to my flat. The only thing I had was music and thank god I did. I would listen to those records and it would remind me of the good old days with Lloyd. My parents died a long time ago and I never had much family to speak of, so the only person I really cared about was Gertrude, Lloyd's wife. I made a promise to look after her – make sure she could pay her rent, bills, all that. She was so tough. Way tougher than me. I mean, Christ, she had a baby to look after and no husband, which is difficult enough as it is. The only thing was that she couldn't bear to keep his name. As soon as he died, she stopped calling herself Mrs McLean. It was too painful a reminder. So she used her maiden name.'

Maiden name? Kofi didn't know what that meant.

'It's the name she had before she was married,' explained Mr Thompson, as though reading Kofi's mind.

'What was it?' asked Kofi.

Mr Thompson clasped his hands together and leaned forward.

'Weaver,' he said quietly.

Weaver?

Mrs Weaver?

There was a pause as everyone let the information sink in. Old Mrs Weaver's dead husband was Mr Thompson's best friend from forty years ago. Kofi's mind was spinning. Mr Thompson took a breath, and carried on.

'So as well as paying my own rent, I found the money to pay for Gertrude's rent and her bills, when I could. She had a child to look after, and I wanted to do more than just offer him cups of tea growing up, you know what I mean?'

He chuckled dryly.

'Everything was fine when I was working regular jobs, but as I got older, it got hard.'

He looked apologetically at Kofi. 'I'm not as young as I used to be.'

Kofi nodded. 'You're very old.'

'Kofi,' said Mum.

Mr Thompson laughed. And then he suddenly became serious. 'You're right,' he said sadly. 'Too old. You get a bit desperate. Everything's so expensive nowadays. So when I was in that shop and all them kids came rushing in, I saw the till and I saw the money and I – I—'

Mr Thompson trailed off, looking down at the floor again. Mum reached a hand over the table and placed it softly on one of his.

'It's OK,' she said gently. 'Thank you – for telling us.'

Emmanuel cleared his throat and Kofi looked up.

Gloria was wiping the inside corners of her eyes. 'Mrs Weaver . . .' she said quietly, processing the whole story.

'I know . . .' Kofi said slowly. 'It's hard to think of her as a young woman.'

Mum stood up to head to the kitchen. 'Everyone starts off young, Kofi. You'll be an old man one day.'

Kofi scrunched his face up. 'But *Mrs Weaver* though. I just can't pic—'

He stopped. A wave of realisation suddenly washed over him. He sprang to his feet, knocking his chair backwards and making Mr Thompson jump. Then he thrust a hand into his back pocket and withdrew the picture he had found at the furniture shop. With eyes stretched wide, he slammed the photograph on the table. Everyone huddled round to look.

'Is that . . .' began Mr Thompson in disbelief. But his reaction said it all. The photograph was indeed a picture of himself, Lloyd McLean and a young Mrs Weaver. It was like staring into a time machine.

'Oh my giddy aunt . . .' whispered Mr Thompson, his eyes scanning the image for every last detail. 'This is just near the old park that used to be off behind the main road. Look at how young I am! Gertrude must have been pregnant here, but only just.'

He looked at Kofi, amazed. 'Where did you get this?'

'I found it,' replied Kofi unhelpfully. Then he asked

a question of his own, his mind scrambling to connect the dots.

'Mrs Weaver's baby,' he started to ask. 'It was a boy, right?'

'That's right,' replied Mr Thompson.

'And what was he called?' pushed Kofi.

Mr Thompson replied immediately. 'She gave him his dad's middle name. To honour his memory.'

He paused.

'Linton.'

39

Making Amends

It was Sunday morning, the day after the big discovery about Linton and Mrs Weaver. Kofi still couldn't quite believe that Linton was actually Mrs Weaver's son. He was itching to dive into the adventure and discover more, but his guilt over the camcorder was really starting to eat away at him. Being in trouble with Mum and Dad was one thing, but Emmanuel's words about breaking their trust made Kofi feel even worse. He had to do something about it. It was time to do the right thing.

Kofi looked at the uneven piles of coins he had stacked in front of him on the foldaway dining table. He'd cleared out all of his secret hiding places to see just how much money he had. It was an impressive stash. Not quite enough to replace a broken camcorder, but maybe enough to make a start.

'I still can't believe that story last night,' said Gloria as she swept into the front room, holding a bowl of cereal. Dad had gone early to church with Emmanuel, and Mum had popped out to see Mrs Weaver. Gloria paused to assess Kofi's tabletop activity. 'What's that? Don't tell me it's homework – I won't believe you.'

Next to Kofi's piles of money was a crumpled piece of paper covered in his scratchy writing. Gloria snatched it up as she passed him.

'Hey!' protested Kofi. Gloria held it away from him and started reading.

'*Dear Mum, dear Dad ...*' she read slowly. '*I know I've let you down. Again. And I really am sorry. I want you to trust me and I don't want to keep getting in trouble any more ...*'

'Gimme!' said Kofi, alarmed. His letter was supposed to be private. Gloria powered on.

'*I have decided to pay you back for the damage I have*

caused. I will give you all my savings and I will sell my Game Boy to make up the rest of . . .'

Gloria trailed off, letting the hand holding the letter fall gently to her side.

'You'll really sell your *Game Boy*?' she asked quietly. 'To get the money you need?'

'*Yes*,' answered Kofi quickly, snatching the letter back. 'I'm taking it into school tomorrow.'

Gloria was momentarily stunned. She knew how much Kofi loved his Game Boy. If he was willing to sacrifice it then he must be really serious about putting things right.

'Anyway,' Kofi continued. 'There's almost twenty pounds there. I'm taking it to Mr Ambrose to get notes, instead of all this change. Then I can put everything in an envelope.'

Mr Ambrose owned a little shop hut on the estate that sold sweets, newspapers, drinks and a few groceries like bread and milk. Kofi knew that he would welcome the loose change because it saved him a trip to the bank.

Gloria looked at her brother with something like a smile appearing on her face. Kofi watched as she came over and carefully took a fifty-pence coin from one of the stacks.

'I'll have a Twix, please,' she said, smiling. She was genuinely proud of what Kofi had decided to do.

Kofi smiled back and took the coin from her fingers.

*

A few minutes later, Kofi was out in the estate making his way to Mr Ambrose's hut, carrying all his coins in his deepest pockets.

'Wha' you wan me to do wid all dis coin, boy?'

Mr Ambrose spoke in a gruff Trinidadian accent. He never bothered with saying hello. Kofi explained what he wanted while the shopkeeper listened with his head cocked at an inquisitive angle.

'So who dis money for?' he asked, opening the till to count Kofi's coins into. 'You?'

Kofi's mouth didn't give his brain the time to make anything up.

'I broke my dad's new camcorder and I'm giving him all of my savings to replace it.'

Mr Ambrose looked down at Kofi with an expression that Kofi couldn't read.

'I'm a really, *really* good son,' said Kofi, blinking.

Mr Ambrose softened visibly. 'You're doin the

right ting, boy,' he said, nodding. 'It's good to tek responsibility for yuh action.'

Suddenly, Mr Ambrose's eyes lit up.

'What wrong wit dis camera anyway?' he asked. 'You nah know me a fully trained electrician?'

Kofi's eyes widened. 'Really?' he asked hopefully.

'Yeah, man!' beamed Mr Ambrose. 'I can fix anyting. Listen, bring da ting to me and mi see what I can do. It's a Sunday – lemme do a likkle good deed one time.'

Kofi's face split into a massive grin.

Less than ten minutes later, he had returned, slightly out of breath, carrying the camcorder, but this time safely encased in its cardboard box. He placed the box on the counter and Mr Ambrose reached in to remove the broken device.

'*Careful*,' said Kofi. Mr Ambrose stopped and gave him a look that could have made a clock stop ticking.

'Uh, c-carry on,' stammered Kofi.

*

'You fixed it?'

Gloria's face was incredulous.

'Not me,' beamed Kofi. 'Mr Ambrose. He said I was doing *a good ting* so he decided to help me out.'

Gloria shook her head in mild disbelief, turning the camcorder over in her hands. It was pretty much good as new, apart from a few scuffs that Mr Ambrose couldn't quite rub out. The main thing was that the broken door was completely fixed, and a few loose panels had been screwed firmly together.

'Kof, you're one lucky so and so, you know that?'

Kofi grinned. 'I deserve it, don't I?'

Gloria rolled her eyes. 'Did you get my Twix?'

Kofi pretended to lick his fingers and rubbed his stomach.

'Yep. It was delicious,' he joked.

40

Finding Linton

Giving the camera back to Dad was the main event that Sunday afternoon. Mum and Dad were clearly impressed with the efforts that Kofi had gone to, and said it was very responsible of him to have written a letter of explanation too. Stern words were exchanged about taking valuable property to school, and Kofi promised to never do anything so silly again. And with the look that Mum gave him, he really meant it.

With the camcorder returned and his curfew over, Kofi felt like a huge weight of guilt had finally been lifted from his shoulders. The very next day at school, Kofi spent all of first break telling Mr Thompson's story to Kelvin, who listened with wide eyes and an open mouth. It was incredible to think of all these hidden pasts and secrets, about people who the boys had ignored for so long.

By lunchtime, Kofi had the beginnings of a plan, which he was starting to explain to Kelvin behind the refectory, amidst rowdy games of tag and football matches with ancient tennis balls. Leroy still wasn't back at school, but Kofi also knew that once his name was cleared, Redge would have to let him back in. Kofi was a kid on a mission.

'We need to speak to Linton,' he said, leaning one foot on the wall behind him.

'Why?' asked Kelvin. It was a reasonable question.

'We know where all the stuff from Clipper FM has ended up – the second-hand furniture shop. We have to tell him and help him get it back,' Kofi said.

Kelvin nodded.

'How do we find him?' asked Kelvin.

'I was thinking you could help with that,' said Kofi hopefully.

Kelvin squinted to the left and chewed the inside of his cheek.

'W-what was his hair like?' asked Kelvin.

Kofi pulled a face. 'Short back and sides. High-top. Why?'

Kelvin thought for a moment.

'Well, don't m-m-most people with a short back and sides get their hair cut, what, once every t-two weeks?'

Kofi started to catch on. Kelvin continued.

'So, i-if Linton is still around, he'll have to go to – to …' He took a deep breath. '… to th-the barber at some point soon, right? And e-everyone around here goes to—'

'Fly Cutz!' interrupted Kofi triumphantly, naming the barbershop on the high street. 'Kelvin, you're a genius!'

The bell rang, signalling the end of lunchtime. Kofi grinned at his friend.

'Let's go find him,' he said, his eyes gleaming. 'I know what we have to do.'

*

The next week and a half was devoted to visiting Fly Cutz barbershop in the hope of catching Linton getting a haircut. Kofi and Kelvin would go there every day after school and in the afternoon on

Saturday, after Kofi had come back from shopping with his mum. They couldn't go inside because it would be weird to sit there without getting a trim, so they loitered on the street. Thankfully, Fly Cutz was just about visible from the minicab office with the arcade machines, so they could play a few rounds of *Street Fighter II* to pass the time while they waited. Besides, they didn't fancy hanging around and getting on Big Tyrone's nerves. Big Tyrone was the Fly Cutz owner – a large Bajan man with thick arms and a short temper. There were infamous stories of him throwing kids out mid-haircut if they got rude. You didn't want to be on his bad side.

Meanwhile, Mr Thompson had told the school about the money. Mum had personally made sure of it, and when she meant business, she wasn't someone to mess around with. Mr Thompson had also given all of the money back to the shop, but Kofi wasn't sure if he'd met with Redge yet. Leroy was nowhere to be seen, and Kofi didn't even know where he lived in the nearby estate, which meant that it was impossible to track him down. The rap battles were still cancelled and no one seemed to want to risk meeting up at the mini-mart at all. Getting expelled obviously wasn't worth it. Memories of Clipper FM were fading fast too. And with no sign of Linton, it felt like a boring new normal was settling in for the winter.

Then, on Friday afternoon: 'Leroy!'

Kofi pointed excitedly, jogging Kelvin's shoulder with his other hand. He was right – it was indeed Leroy, strolling out of the chicken shop as if he hadn't been gone at all, eating casually out of a box of chips. Kofi and Kelvin abandoned their game and trotted over.

'Coinboy! Reloader!' Leroy greeted them both with a grin. They all touched fists, Kofi adding a few extra made-up secret handshake moves along the way.

'Where you been, man?' asked Kofi, rattling off a few more questions. 'You coming back to school? What you doing here?'

Leroy smoothed the back of his neck with one hand and chose which question to answer first. 'They sent me Stanford, innit,' he said, staring into nowhere.

'Stanford?' said Kelvin and Kofi together. Stanford was the name of a notorious pupil referral school. It was one step away from a young offenders' unit, and after that, the next step was prison. Leroy had already been on his final warning at St Campions, so lashing out at the head teacher, plus the accusation of stealing from the shop, had tipped him over the edge.

'Yeah, man,' said Leroy. 'It was calm still, but man

was always *fighting* in there. And no one had any bars or nothing.'

Kofi suddenly noticed the faint traces of a fading bruise around Leroy's left eye. Stanford couldn't have been *that* calm.

Kofi thought about asking Leroy what had really happened to him while he'd been away, but the moment came and went.

'Now my name's cleared, I'm back on ends, innit,' Leroy continued with a flex of the shoulder and a smirk. 'Home for *good*. Anyway, what are you man doing out on road?'

Kofi thumbed in the direction of Fly Cutz. 'Remember that pirate radio station?' he said. 'I need to speak to Linton – the guy that runs it.'

'The one that doesn't exist, yeah?' said Leroy playfully. Kofi rolled his eyes and Leroy turned his attention to Kelvin.

'Ey, Kels, you been writing?' he asked hopefully. Kofi could instantly tell that Leroy had missed his rapping buddy, but he didn't feel the slightest pang of jealousy.

'Well …' said Kelvin, his face lighting up as he reached slowly into his satchel. He pulled out a handful of loose-leaf pages and shook them gently.

'Yes!' exclaimed Leroy. 'Lemme see …'

The boys crowded round Kelvin's lyrics and …
Linton strolled right past them on his way down the
high street. None of the boys looked up.

A few moments later, Linton doubled back.

'Yo, excuse me …' he said in his low, lazy drawl.

Kofi, Kelvin and Leroy looked up. Linton pointed
straight at Kofi.

'Ain't you that kid who spit bars on Clipper that
time?' he said. His voice was warm and friendly with
recognition. Kofi was momentarily stunned.

'*Linton?*' said Kelvin and Leroy at the same time.

'Yes!' cried Kofi. He turned to Leroy. 'See? He does
exist.' Then he turned to Linton and blurted out the
first thing that came into his head. 'Are you getting
your hair cut today?'

Linton looked at Kofi with two raised eyebrows, too
surprised to do anything but answer truthfully.

'Uh, nah,' he replied. 'Tomorrow. Afternoon.'

'Doesn't matter,' rushed Kofi, arms flapping.
'Listen, we know all about the radio station. We
know where your equipment is too. It's all at the
furniture shop where my brother works. We can get
it back, man. We have to do something. We can save
Clipper FM!'

Kofi wisely chose not to reveal what he knew about

Mrs Weaver, Mr Thompson and Linton's past. That could come later.

Linton was shocked by this wave of information. But then his face settled back into place: cool and expressionless.

'Nah, bro,' he said with a sigh. 'Once they catch you doing pirate, it's over, man. Too risky.' He thrust his hands into his deep leather pockets. 'I'm out.'

Kofi's face fell. He was crushed.

'Sorry, man,' said Linton apologetically. 'But stay good, yeah.' He offered a fist, which Kofi reluctantly spudded with his own. With a final nod at all three boys, Linton flicked the collar of his jacket and sauntered off down the main road.

'That went well,' said Leroy sarcastically.

Kofi kicked at the ground in frustration. He had hoped that Linton would spring into action and join the quest to save the secret radio station. In his head, he had pictured all the equipment being put back together and everyone having a happily ever after. But Linton's reaction meant that was just not going to happen.

'Come on, man,' said Leroy, as if he could read Kofi's mind. 'Let's go Junction and hang out.'

Kofi shook his head sadly. He wasn't in the mood. 'I'm going home . . .' he said flatly.

'Wait a s-second ...'

Kelvin's interruption made Kofi and Leroy swivel their heads in his direction. Kelvin was turning through the pages of his little red notebook, which he had produced from his bag.

'... maybe we *should* go to the Junction.' Kelvin pointed at a list of names written in his neat handwriting. 'I've had an idea.'

41

Shanice Refuses to Help

'No way.'

Shanice was perched on a tall stool in the food court, delicately holding a chip between the finger and thumb of one hand. Her friend Tanya was sitting next to her. The boys had found her at the Junction, just as Kelvin had suspected. Kofi had gone to try and talk her round to a new plan while Kelvin and Leroy had been trying to find the rappers from the car park cyphers. That was part one of the big new plan. But Shanice wasn't having it.

Kofi fell to his knees in front of Shanice and clasped his hands together in a desperate fist.

'Get up off the floor, man,' snapped Shanice, glancing around in case anyone was looking.

'Pleeease, Shanice,' begged Kofi, clambering to his feet. 'And can I have a chip?'

'No, you cannot have a chip,' scowled Shanice, kissing her teeth. 'I haven't forgotten the last time you had a bright idea. We almost got arrested, you little bean-head.'

'Yeah but – no but – yeah but—' Kofi was floundering helplessly. At that moment, Leroy appeared from the crowds, approaching the area where Shanice was sitting.

'Sorry, man,' he said to Kofi with a shrug. 'No luck.'

'Oh, it's *him* ...' said Tanya with a huge fold of the arms. Then she spotted Kelvin at Leroy's side and instantly melted. 'And *him*!' she squealed, clutching at her heart with both fists.

'H-hey,' said Kelvin.

'Awww ...' the girls whimpered, leaning their heads to one side. Leroy scratched his head. Kofi powered on.

'It's not even my bright idea!' he spluttered, still trying to convince Shanice to change her mind. 'It's Kelvin's!'

Shanice paused. 'Oh, for real?' Her face broke into a smile. 'Why didn't you say so, man? He's the clever one, innit? If it's his plan we'll probably be all right. Yeah, I'll help you.'

Everyone looked at Kelvin, who didn't quite know what to say.

'Um, thank you?' he said hesitantly.

'Awww ...' whimpered the girls again.

'OK then,' said Shanice, snapping to attention and clapping her hands together. 'Let's get to work.'

Then to Kelvin:

'You still got that notebook?'

42

Fly Cutz

Saturday morning dragged on forever as Kofi waited impatiently for the afternoon. All morning long, he twitched and tapped, trying, and failing, to hurry time along. By the time he was back from shopping with Mum and briefly catching up with Mrs Weaver on the stairs, he could barely contain himself. He was busy chucking food into cupboards at breakneck speed so that he could go out and meet Kelvin and Leroy, as he had promised. Emmanuel was already at work and Gloria was 'doing coursework' at Shanice's place.

'You OK there?' said Mum as Kofi stuffed a plastic bag full of scotch bonnet peppers into the cutlery drawer.

'Yes, Mum, gotta go!' he rattled back, tearing out of the kitchen.

She called after him. 'OK, but I won't be back when you get in so don't forget your—'

BANG. The door slammed shut.

'—key.'

Kofi took the steps four at a time as he flew down the stairwells, pulling his jacket on as he went. Downstairs, Kelvin and Leroy were already waiting by the dilapidated picnic tables.

'Seven minutes and ... forty-three seconds,' said Kelvin, looking at his watch. 'I win.'

'Win what?' said Kofi, zipping up his jacket.

'We were making bets about how late you'd be,' said Leroy, handing a chocolate bar over to Kelvin.

'Hey!' said Kofi. 'I'm never late!'

'You're *always* late,' replied Leroy. Kelvin was nodding.

'It's true,' he said. 'Y-you are.'

Kofi was indignant. 'Tell me one time I was late,' he demanded.

'Just now,' said Kelvin, taking a nibble of his chocolate.

Kofi kissed his teeth. 'Come on, man, let's go.'

A short walk later, the three boys were on the high street outside Fly Cutz. There was a thin bustle on the streets and even though it wasn't dark, lights were starting to come on in most shop windows.

'Look!' said Kofi in a husky whisper. 'There he is!'

He pointed through the door of Fly Cutz. Linton was sitting in the waiting area on a black leather sofa. He was deep in conversation with a man in a baseball cap next to him while the barbers were busy cutting. A small, boxy television was on in the corner but no one was paying any attention to it. Every chair was full and Big Tyrone was working up a sweat trying to get through his regulars. Saturday was the barbershop's busiest day.

'I'll do the talking,' whispered Kofi. He pointed to himself with the flat of his hand and turned to each of his friends. 'I'm the best talker, you see.'

He walked towards the shop before they had a chance to respond.

Kofi pushed the heavy glass door open and all eyes momentarily swung in his direction. For a short second, all that could be heard was the buzz of clippers and the static of the television. Then everyone returned to what they were doing, ignoring the twelve-year-old boy standing nervously at the door. Big Tyrone spoke over the sound of his clippers, not looking up.

'Tirty minutes,' he said gruffly. 'Tek a seat over dere.'

Kofi didn't speak or move. Frowning, Big Tyrone clicked off his clippers and looked up at Kofi.

'You nah hear me?' he said roughly. He pointed with the clippers. '*Siddown.*'

Kofi blinked. He cleared his throat nervously. 'I— I wanted to, to speak with . . .'

'Best talker, yeah . . .' said Leroy quietly to Kelvin.

'I wanted to speak with – with *him*,' finished Kofi.

He pointed at Linton, who, for the first time, looked up from his conversation. Kofi saw him close his eyes and roll his head backwards at the neck, muttering something under his breath. Kofi's heart sank. And then Linton stood up.

'Listen, my yute,' he began, arms opening. 'I told you yesterday: I can't be dealing with that stuff no more. I know you enjoyed it and yeah, it ain't fair that it's all over, but it's too risky, you get me?'

'What "stuff" you taak bout?' said Big Tyrone in a unique combination of annoyance and alarm. 'You comin to taak some shady business in *my* shop? Eh?'

Kofi put both hands out in front of him.

'No, no!' he cried. 'It's nothing like that. It's about a

257

radio station. Clipper FM. It used to be on the estate but it all got taken away.' His passion was making him fluent. 'That radio station is part of my life. It's part of all our lives. The estate just isn't the same without it. And I think I know how we can get it back on air.'

Kofi carried on. 'You saved me once, Linton, I remember that. And now it's *my* turn to save *you*.'

Linton was stunned into silence. For moment, Kofi thought he'd convinced him, but then that impassive look returned to Linton's face. He replied in his slow drawl as he sat back down.

'Sorry, my g,' he said slowly. 'I can't do it.'

A few murmurs started to rise up from the men getting their haircuts. A woman braiding hair looked at Kofi with sympathetic eyes. But Kofi had a gleam in his.

'I thought you might say that . . .' he said mysteriously. Then he leaned back towards the door and called out to Kelvin and Leroy.

'Now!'

Big Tyrone clicked his clippers off again and put his hands on his hips. 'Now, what on eart is gwannin up in here . . .'

Before he could get an answer, Leroy put two fingers to his mouth and blew an ear-piercing whistle that shot through the high street. One barber wearing a green bandana flinched at the sound and accidentally buzzed a zero straight through a poor customer's hair. Out of nowhere, a flock of kids appeared, heading in a disorderly line straight for Fly Cutz. Kelvin had his book out, checking names. They were rappers – all the kids who had wanted to be on Clipper FM, and a few more. Many were carrying bits and pieces of electrical equipment of all shapes and sizes. Cables, amps, boxes with knobs and switches, microphones. But most were struggling with armfuls of records on twelve-inch vinyl, hundreds in total, in bags and crates that needed two people to carry them because they were so heavy.

Ushering them along was Shanice, flanked by Gloria and Tanya, with satisfied smiles on their faces. With only a few hours' notice, Shanice had somehow managed to get them all together. The plan was in action.

'I didn't think you'd want to go back to the radio station,' said Kofi with a grin. 'So I thought I'd bring the radio station to *you*.'

Everyone in the shop was now hooked on this mad unfolding drama, not least of all Linton, who now looked like he was in a dream that he couldn't quite shake himself awake from. Kofi opened the glass door wide. There were more kids than he could count, all spilling on to the main road.

'There's a few more coming with the big stuff,' said Shanice, patting the baby curls on the side of her temple.

Linton stepped forward to have a closer look. He couldn't believe his eyes. At that point, the voice of Ryu Spitter could be heard huffing and puffing through the crowd. He was leading a small group of Year 11s, carrying 'the big stuff' to the front. It was a collection of speakers.

'Ey, move, man,' grumbled Ryu Spitter, struggling with one end of a huge speaker. 'This is heavy, y'know!'

Linton was in shock. 'Yo . . . but how did . . . ?'

Kofi's face stretched into a smile.

'These are all the rappers who wanted to pay subs to be on Clipper FM,' he explained happily. 'We got them together, and all their subs' money, and used it to buy back all your radio stuff from the second-hand furniture shop where my brother works.'

Linton's jaw fell open.

'It was easy,' finished Kofi, still grinning.

'Was it now?' interrupted Shanice with a fold of the arms. She'd spent most of the previous day using her network to get everyone together.

'Um, Shanice did most of the work,' admitted Kofi quickly.

'Now wholl on just one minute!'

Big Tyrone's voice boomed through the shop, making everyone jump. The barber with the green bandana flinched again, putting another wild line into his customer's hair. Big Tyrone slammed his clippers down on the counter.

'Yuh mean to say that dis pickney here done gone roun up all him likkle friend, put them likkle money together to go and buy up *aaaall* dis sound system, then come here, to *my* shop, on mi *busiest* day, to come plug up de whol ting on *aaaall* mi 'lectrical socket and bring my man's radio to life while me try run business and cut HAIR??'

Big Tyrone's voice had risen gradually until the last word was screamed at a decibel-shaking shout. Everyone was looking at him, and he was staring straight at a very nervous Kofi. Kofi swallowed a dry gulp.

'What a *wicked* idea!' said Big Tyrone with a sudden, warm smile. 'You got any reggae?'

43

Party Time at the Barbershop

The next fifteen minutes were spent in a state of mild chaos as Linton, Kofi, everyone in the barbershop and the hordes of kids outside began setting up an impromptu sound system in Fly Cutz. Thankfully, T from the estate had been passing by and Kofi called him over to help. T had a fantastic memory for all things technical and was an instant help to Linton, putting all the cables together. A few of the older customers started trading stories about setting up parties 'back in the day', while some of the rappers started trading bars in a little warm-up for the main event. Linton and T took up residence to one side of the main entrance, calling for different pieces of kit from the crowd outside. The big speakers went out to the front on the other side of the entrance.

There was a funny moment when Ibby from Year 9 at St Campions arrived, on his own, carrying a whole table. It was the one with a brass handle on the front, next to a deep, diagonal scratch, like a scar. Ibby had picked it up from the second-hand furniture shop and half dragged it the whole way. Panting with the effort, he planted the table by the entrance, before sliding to the ground with his head against the glass and two thumbs sticking weakly up.

Kofi was beside himself with excitement. The whole thing had the atmosphere of a big event ready to happen.

Soon enough, the turntables were set up and Linton was ready to drop the needle on a record spinning slowly on its platter. There was the faint crackle of static, and then ... *Bu-KAP, Boom boom KAP, Badoom!* A beautiful reggae drum roll kicked into gear. A cheer went up that was almost drowned out by the sound of reggae pulsing through Linton's set-up. Yep. The party was definitely on.

'Mi love dis song!' shouted Big Tyrone over the music, swaying side to side and touching fists with Linton. They laughed and Linton looked over to where Kofi was standing with Kelvin.

'You're one mad yute, you know that?' he said with a slow shake of the head. 'But for real, thank you, man.'

'You're welcome!' Kofi beamed.

*

Everyone lost all track of time as late afternoon turned into early evening. Linton was an expert DJ and somehow managed to get everyone dancing to everything he chose, making different styles of music blend into each other like streams meeting at the mouths of rivers. It wasn't long before the microphone was set up and all the MCs finally had their chance to spit bars on Clipper FM, even though Linton wasn't broadcasting. They came up in twos and threes, sometimes fours or more, letting fly with volley after volley of lyrical wordplay. Necks were straining with intensity and crowds of kids were shouting their support whenever a good punchline hit. Every now and again, someone said something so good that Linton or T would pull back the record and reload it, while everyone shouted their support. A huge cheer went up when Leroy and Kelvin jumped on the mic with their back-to-back flows, which had everyone hopping from foot to foot. But the biggest reload happened when Big Tyrone jumped on the mic to deliver some warbling, high-pitched reggae singing. After that, he was so happy that he handed over a few notes and sent some kids to the local shop to get snacks and drinks. It was truly a party to remember.

By this point, Ibby's table had come in handy as a stand for another big speaker, and the party was fully spilling out into the high street. Cars and buses were slowing down to see what all the commotion was and a local Caribbean food hut had started selling Jamaican patties.

At first, no one noticed the old man in the red scarf who was watching the scene from a passing bus along the main road. Curious, he got off at his stop and drifted towards the barber's. That's when Gloria spotted him. It was Mr Thompson. She quickly found Kofi and pointed him out. They watched on.

Mr Thompson walked slowly through the crowds, stopping near the Fly Cutz entrance as he noticed some of the older equipment. Then he spotted a familiar face.

'Linton!' he cried, his face breaking into a smile. 'What's all this then!'

Linton looked up from his workstation and removed a pair of headphones from his head.

'Uncle Jim …' he said in a welcoming drawl. Then he pointed at Kofi. 'Long story,' he said with a chuckle.

Then Linton and Mr Thompson exchanged a hearty handshake that turned into a warm hug.

'You looking after your mother, yeah?' asked Mr Thompson, gripping Linton by the shoulder.

'Course,' Linton replied.

Kofi was amazed. He knew they knew each other, but seeing them like this was mind-blowing. There was a passing gleam in Linton's eye as he reached into a crate, pulled out a small seven-inch record and cued it up on an empty turntable. Moments later, the sounds of smooth calypso filled the air, drawing a few cheers from some of the elders.

'Your dad would've loved this,' said Mr Thompson quietly to Linton, wiping his eye. 'He bloody loved a knees-up, I'm telling you.'

Gloria bit her lip and Kofi felt a lump in his throat.

Linton's face morphed into a happy smile.

'Let's run some tunes,' he grinned.

*

The party was going strong when Kofi suddenly heard the unmistakable sound of someone calling his name, just before he was about to be in trouble.

'Kofi!'

Kofi and Gloria looked up.

'Dad!'

Gloria disappeared into the crowds, leaving Kofi to fend for himself.

Dad knew his son. He knew by instinct that whatever was going on here, Kofi was somehow responsible. And it clearly had nothing to do with school or church. With Dad being out at work so much, he tended to be out of the loop on things that were going on at home. This situation was no exception.

'Dad, I can explain,' Kofi lied. And then Mr Thompson stepped in.

'This your boy?' he asked Dad, pointing at Kofi.

Dad was taken aback. 'Yes,' he said. 'Yes, he is.'

Mr Thompson took one of Dad's hands in both of his and shook it energetically. 'That's one great kid you've got there,' he said. 'You should be so proud of him.'

Mr Thompson gestured around at the scene, catching sight of Leroy. Kofi noticed his eyes widen slightly, as if he'd just had an idea.

'Be right back . . .' said Mr Thompson mysteriously,

disappearing out of the shop with a quick goodbye to the group.

Dad was visibly shocked.

'Does your mum know about this?' he asked Kofi.

'Yes . . . ?' said Kofi. It was a half lie. She did know about Mr Thompson, at least.

'And Emmanuel?' asked Dad.

'He helped!' lied Kofi.

Dad's face softened into a smile. He looked around at the happy faces and joyous scene, taking it all in. Then he put an arm around Kofi's shoulder, his lips stretched wide. He wasn't sure why, but he knew that Kofi had done a good thing here.

'Well done, son,' he said. 'You know, the church could do with a new events organiser . . .'

Before Kofi had a chance to reply, Mr Thompson had appeared again. But this time he had a surprise guest with him.

'Clapman!' exclaimed Kofi.

Clapman smiled. 'The name's Sharif,' he said warmly, extending a hand to shake.

Kofi turned to Dad to start to explain. 'He runs the shop near school with . . .'

'. . . with my dad,' said Sharif. 'Listen, I owe you an apology. And your friend. He here?'

Leroy was currently on the mic, up next to Ibby's table. He was rapping enthusiastically over a sped-up breakbeat instrumental that T had put on. Kofi pointed him out and beckoned him over. Taking his chance for a breather, Leroy loped over, looking at the unlikely group with a cautious expression on his face.

'I've come to apologise,' said Mr Thompson after a deep breath, his brow furrowed. Leroy was taken aback. He could tell the old man meant it.

'Me too,' added Clapman. 'Mr Thompson here explained everything. I was wrong to accuse you of taking the money.'

Mr Thompson looked down at the ground, with his lips in a tight grimace. Clapman continued. 'For real, I'm proper sorry for that.'

Leroy was lost for words. He blinked twice. He wasn't at all used to adults treating him fairly like this.

'It's cause you're so loud, man!' laughed Clapman, breaking the tension with a warm chuckle. Leroy's face broke into a smile.

'Thanks, man,' he said simply.

Clapman clapped one time and extended his arms in a welcoming gesture. 'Listen,' he began. 'Anything you want for this little party in here, you name it. It's yours.

Crisps, sweets, fizzy drink. I'll head back and pick it up right now. My gift.'

Leroy's eyes lit up, exchanging a look of disbelief with Kofi. This was turning into the best day ever. He was just about to respond to Clapman's generous offer when—

WEEUW!

A siren cut through the air. Kofi felt his heart knocking at his ribs and the blood instantly drain from his face.

WEEUW!

It was the police.

44

Ibby's Broken Table

'Aw, man, not this again . . .' sighed Ryu Spitter into the microphone.

There was a violent record scratch as the music abruptly stopped. It was only a single police car, but that was enough to put everyone on guard. Guilty looks started to be exchanged. Kofi tried to make himself as small as possible.

'Right, who's in charge here,' growled the first officer. With a sinking heart, Kofi realised it was the same one who had got in their faces that time with Shanice and the subs rappers. Following close behind was the smaller one with freckles, who, Kofi noticed, looked very uncomfortable about the whole thing.

Big Tyrone stood tall in the middle of the shop and kissed his teeth long and loud. He didn't look scared at all.

'*Me*,' he said firmly. No one else spoke. The growler went straight up to him, looking at him eye to eye.

'And do you realise you're causing a social disturbance, mate?'

Something in the mood changed and Kofi was suddenly very happy that his dad was nearby. Big Tyrone kissed his teeth again.

'Mi not your mate, *mate*,' he said with clear disdain.

The growler held his stare for a few moments, then started walking slowly through the scene. People parted as he approached.

'*This*,' he said with slow relish, 'is an unauthorised gathering. An *illegal*, unauthorised gathering.'

He made eye contact with as many people as possible as he spoke. It was intimidating.

'*And*,' he added, gently knocking at a speaker with his fist. 'It's noise pollution.'

PC Freckles looked like he wanted the ground to swallow him up.

A few grumbles of discontent started among the crowd and Growler put up a hand to silence them. He was at the front of the shop, next to the microphone stand and a group of young rappers gathered by Ibby's table.

'Obstructing a public footpath ...' he continued, tapping at the table with his foot. As he did so, one of its ancient legs gave way and the speaker resting on its surface clattered towards the ground. Leroy and a couple of others barely managed to catch it in time.

'Oi, watch it, man!' shouted Ryu Spitter.

'Quiet!' snapped the growler.

'My table!' cried Ibby, rushing forward to assess the damage.

But it was too late. The table was definitely broken, splintered across its joints and split through the panelling.

That was the moment that everything suddenly erupted into noise and activity. There was a clamour of voices complaining about what the police were doing, and what they weren't doing, while the two officers started raising their hands to try and calm everyone down. The party had turned into scowls, pointed fingers, arguments and people talking over each other.

WEEUW!

Another siren sounded nearby, meaning that more police were on the way. It would be a bad idea to try and run away now.

It was in all this mess that Kofi spotted something out of the corner of his eye. He quickly found Kelvin in the crowd and beckoned him over. Kelvin had spotted it too – a sliver of white poking out from the split panels of Ibby's broken table.

The two boys crouched down to ankle height to take a closer look. Kofi reached out and slowly withdrew it between forefinger and thumb.

'It's paper,' he said. 'Letters.'

He unfolded the crumpled stack of sheets and tried to smooth them out. They had clearly been stuck behind the drawer for a long time. Kelvin leaned in for a better look. After a moment or so, Kofi gave up and flapped the thin sheets in Kelvin's direction.

'I don't understand a word of it,' he said distractedly, looking up at Dad, who was side by side with Big Tyrone arguing about something or other with the growler.

'Wow,' said Kofi, both shocked and impressed. 'Go on, Dad!'

Meanwhile, Kelvin had taken the sheets of paper and was squinting at them intently.

'Hey, Kofi,' he whispered. 'I think these might be . . . important . . .'

Kofi wasn't listening. He was too busy trying to work out if Dad was about to get in serious trouble or not.

'Look,' said Kelvin, pointing at one of the pages. Kofi dragged his eyes away from Dad and Big Tyrone to have a look.

'Deeds . . . of . . . ownership . . .' he read slowly.

'Yeah, so?'

'I don't really understand all of it . . .' said Kelvin, turning through the pages. 'But . . .' He suddenly looked up. 'Your dad!' he said brightly. 'He studied accountancy and law w-when he was at university! I remember you telling Miss Hill in the first maths lesson in Year Seven.'

'Did he? Did I?' Kofi looked at his friend and wondered if Kelvin ever actually forgot *anything*.

Kelvin had already started making his way over to Kofi's dad, who was in the middle of high-fiving and side-hugging Big Tyrone. They were both clearly enjoying having a standing debate with local law enforcement. A small crowd had gathered to watch the show.

Looking up, Kelvin tapped Kofi's dad on the arm, before handing him the sheets of paper, pointing at a few choice lines. Turning away from the argument for a second, Kofi's dad leaned forward to peer at the papers.

'Because *we* –' Big Tyrone pointed at his heaving chest – 'have *rights*!' His huge belly stuck out proudly. 'And *you* come here with nuthin but *wrongs*!'

A small cheer went up and Big Tyrone started shaking hands and touching fists like a local hero.

'Wait a minute . . .' whispered Dad, flicking through the pages he'd just been given. He was tapping frantically on Big Tyrone's shoulder while looking around the shop at the same time.

'One second,' smiled Big Tyrone, who was right in the middle of telling the police where to go.

'Rah . . . !' said Ryu Spitter.

'This is jokes!' said Leroy.

'Alie!' said Shanice.

'*Tyrone . . .*' hissed Dad.

The noise continued. Dad tried again, this time to everyone.

'*Excuse me!*' he shouted.

'That's his church voice,' Kofi said knowingly to Kelvin.

Dad's church voice was loud enough to make

everyone stop and look. Dad turned to face Officer Growler and PC Freckles. He held up the papers in his hand.

'I think you'll want to hear this.'

42 Years Earlier

'Me tell you, Jimmy, dis been a *dream* of mine since I was a likkle bwoy!'

The high-rise block of flats was brand-new, standing tall and proud, windows gleaming in the sun. The surrounding estate was leafy and spacious. Quiet sounds of life could be heard fluttering in the background. People chatting, the rumble of a bus from the nearby high street, brooms sweeping pavements ... A few British flags were flapping in the breeze, attached to branches of trees with string. It had been a few weeks since the coronation of the new queen, but people were still celebrating.

The two men paused to look up at the impressive building towering above. Lloyd waved his papers high in the air and, with his other arm, hugged his friend triumphantly. Jimmy grinned. He was happy to be helping his friend.

'Seriously, Jim,' continued Lloyd, stashing the papers safely in his inside pocket. 'Thank you so much fe let me use your address for the licence. I'll get it changed soon as me get that big new house for me and Gertrude, ya hear mi?'

'And the baby!' laughed James. 'You're about to be a father now!'

Lloyd paused to look up at the clear blue afternoon sky, shaking his head in vague disbelief. 'You're right...' he said wistfully. 'And me cyan hardly believe it – me very own pickney! Watch how me teach him all about sound system and ting. Him gwan be a *big* soundboy, just like him farda, trust!'

'Oh, so it's a boy then?' joked James. 'You reading the future now?'

'Of course!' Lloyd patted his inside pocket. 'And I already left aaall me equipment to him.'

He threw a cheeky look at James.

'Which I know my good friend James Thompson is happy to look after for me . . .'

James grinned. His new flat was already filling up with all sorts of kit for playing music. After only a few weeks since moving in, it looked more like a studio workshop than a cosy home. But that was how he liked it.

'Here we are,' said James, looking up at the block of flats. 'Top floor. Hope your legs are feeling fit.'

'Race you!' said Lloyd suddenly, and the two men scampered towards the stairwell like boys at the end-of-school-bell.

'I . . . win . . .' panted James, standing outside the flat with his hands on his knees.

'On . . .ly . . . cah . . . me . . . let you . . .' replied Lloyd, through puffs and wheezes.

Inside the flat, Lloyd collapsed into an armchair and unfolded the papers from his inside pocket.

'Drink?' said James, leaning in from the kitchen.

'Rum?' asked Lloyd.

'Even better,' replied James, holding out a tin. 'Yorkshire Tea. The best cuppa in the world.'

Lloyd chuckled. 'When me start throw parties, you can bring the bar!'

He looked around the room.

'Where can I put this – for safekeeping?' he called over the sound of a boiling kettle.

'The old table,' called James. 'With the drawer – and the scratch on it.'

Lloyd looked around. He found the table and pulled the drawer open by its brass handle, placing the papers inside. The drawer stuck slightly when he tried to push it shut, so he had to jiggle it about until it closed. Then James appeared, holding two steaming mugs.

'Cheers,' he grinned happily. 'Now, let me show you this new amplifier I've been working on . . .'

45

Back on Air

'So wait – you're telling me that the radio station was *legal* all along?'

Emmanuel's face looked like a jigsaw puzzle with all the pieces scrambled together.

'YES,' said Kofi and Gloria at the same time.

It was Sunday morning and the three siblings were in the front room. Gloria and Kofi were catching Emmanuel up on what had happened. Or at least they were trying to.

'I – what – but ...' Emmanuel was lost.

'And this guy's supposed to be going to *university* next year,' said Kofi to Gloria, thumbing in his brother's direction.

Gloria took a deep breath. 'OK, from the beginning,' she breathed. 'Lloyd McLean—'

'Linton's *dad*,' interrupted Kofi.

Gloria continued. 'Yes, Linton's dad had a licence to play live music back in the 1950s.'

Emmanuel nodded.

'But the legal paperwork also said that the licence would allow *broadcast transmission* from any premises that were also owned by the licence holder.'

'And that's the radio station,' said Emmanuel, keeping up.

'Wow, you're clever,' quipped Kofi sarcastically.

'Shut up, Kof,' said Gloria. 'Now,' she carried on, 'Linton's flat *actually* belongs to James Thompson ...'

'Mr Thompson!' exclaimed Emmanuel. Kofi clapped an exasperated hand on his forehead.

'Correct,' said Gloria. 'But Mr Thompson has pretty much given the flat to Linton over the years, as a favour to Lloyd and Mrs Weaver. He doesn't live there, but he lets Linton use it for Clipper FM.'

'And Lloyd McLean and Mrs Weaver are Linton's parents ...' said Emmanuel.

'*Exactly*,' said Gloria patiently. 'Which means that the pirate radio station, operating out of that flat, has been legal all along. But the paperwork got stuck behind a drawer—'

'For, like, forty years,' interrupted Kofi. 'Until I found it when the feds broke Ibby's table.' He pointed at himself and beamed with pride.

Gloria pulled a face. '*Anyway*,' she continued. 'This means that the flat has been returned to Mr Thompson, and Linton, because they hadn't been breaking any laws.'

'They're getting some special *condensation* too,' said Kofi wisely.

'Com*pen*sation,' corrected Gloria. 'Money back from the council for being wrongly convicted. Dad's helping them sort it out.'

They all paused to let the size of the story sink in.

'Wow,' said Emmanuel finally. 'You know, it's hard to work out who the hero is. Is it Mr Thompson, for keeping the flat all these years …? Or Linton, for keeping his dad's dream alive …? Or Mum, for confronting Mr Thompson …?'

'Or Dad, for working out all the legal stuff …' suggested Gloria. 'Or the rappers, for buying back all the equipment … Or Big Tyrone … Or—'

'Or me!' said Kofi with a puff of the chest. 'For finding the papers in Ibby's broken table!'

Gloria and Emmanuel rolled their eyes.

'Yep,' Kofi grinned. 'I'm *definitely* the hero.'

Epilogue

We came with a plan and we'll see that through
Who came to win? That's me, not you
Campions boys – we're the Cs up crew
The best MCs and we mean that too.
Clipper FM, yeah, we're so live!
Counting these bars two, three, four, five
We're up in the flats but we climb so high
Make an MC say 'Me oh my!'

Three, four, five to the four, five, six
When T's on the decks you adore that mix
Make no mistake, no pause, no fix
Then get a new tape to record those hits
Audience can't get bored of this
But when you perform they're bored and stiff
Yes we were born with lyrical gifts
It's like your birthday whenever we spit!

It was Saturday afternoon and the regular Clipper FM cypher was in session. Ibby and Little B were going back-to-back and getting serious reloads, with Kelvin and Leroy up next. Kofi was on the radio mic, acting as a compère for the St Campions set while Linton showed T some new tricks on the decks. Kofi loved hyping everyone up and introducing new songs. He said ridiculous things that made everyone roll their eyes, but his energy was infectious. He was in his element. Saturday afternoon cyphers were his favourite part of the week.

As a thank-you to all the rappers who had used their subs money to buy back his equipment, Linton had given them all regular slots to come and cypher, live on air. This meant that every Saturday, the flat was invaded by local kids ready to spit bars. It was electric. Everyone would turn up with fresh lyrics and drink cups of Yorkshire Tea while Linton and T played instrumentals to rhyme over. Already, Clipper FM was getting a reputation for being the best station to hear fresh new talent, as well as a whole range of black musical genres: including R & B, dance hall, reggae, jungle and hip-hop. And it was all happening from the very same estate where Kofi lived.

The flat felt different from the time Kofi had first

visited. It was more alive now, buzzing with the energy of so many people. There were tables set up where rappers could sit and write, and every corner crackled with excitement.

'OK, listening crew!' Kofi boomed into the studio microphone. 'Up next is a little something for all you wobbly old-timers out there . . .'

'Oi!' said Mr Thompson from the other side of the room. He was always at Clipper FM these days, helping out as a radio engineer. He turned out to be a skilful music producer too, helping the kids to piece together beats on some new production gear that Linton had invested in.

'Um, all you older . . . folk . . .' tried Kofi, correcting himself. He signalled over to T, who blew the dust off an old record, before putting it on the platter and gently lowering the needle. There was a fraction of a pause, and then . . . the room was filled with the sounds of calypso, tinkling like sunshine through the air.

Kofi took off his headphones, ready to make his way over to Kelvin, Leroy and the others. But before he did, he paused to take it all in – the music, the people, the atmosphere, everything. The secret radio station wasn't a secret any more. Smiling, he wondered who might be tuning in out there. Then he shook the thought from his mind and headed over to his friends.

*

Back at home, Gloria turned the volume up on the stereo. Mrs Weaver clapped her hands in delight.

'Oooh, me nah heard this one for *years*!' she cried. 'Show me your good foot!'

She stood up, seizing Mum by both hands. In no time the two women were twirling each other around.

'Come, Gloria,' said Mrs Weaver, wobbling left to right with a huge grin on her face. 'Don't think you can get away with not joining in!'

And the three of them danced away together for the whole song.

*

In a small flat near St Campions school, Mr Downfield, Kofi's English teacher, put his pen down for a second and looked at the radio in mild disbelief. When Kofi had told him that he would be on the radio this weekend, Mr Downfield hadn't quite believed him.

Kofi said a lot of things, many of which Mr Downfield had learned to take with a pinch of salt.

Mr Downfield smiled at the sound of Kofi's voice. Somehow, it was true. This charismatic kid in Year 8 really was on the radio. Nodding to himself, Mr Downfield made a silent promise to start up Rap Club again.

*

Shanice was just about to hit the 'stop' button on her cassette recorder, having finished recording all of the St Campions cypher set. She had a full collection of radio cassette tapes, neatly labelled in blue biro and organised chronologically, on a shelf in her immaculately tidy room. She shook her head fondly at the sound of Kofi's voice, wondering what else her best friend's crazy little brother might get her into.

Then, when the calypso tune began to chime through the speaker, she paused. It was nice. Shanice withdrew her hovering finger, and let the recording carry on.

*

The police station common room only had a few people in it, catching a quick break between shifts. The young, freckle-faced officer went over to a small radio in the corner and turned the dial towards the frequency he had written down in his little notebook. He instantly recognised the young, animated voice that was introducing the next song.

'What's that you listening to?' asked a grey-haired officer, stopping to listen.

PC Freckles looked up.

'Oh, nothing,' he said with a smile. 'Just a bit of radio.'

*

The lights changed to green and the minicab lurched forward in the Saturday traffic.

The passenger in the back seat was in the middle of explaining why he hated catching buses. The driver was only half-listening, nodding and making agreeing noises in the right places. Then the driver heard what he was listening for on the tinny car radio.

'Sorry – sorry!' he said, interrupting the passenger's flow. 'Listen!'

The driver put the volume up on the sound of a boy's

voice saying something about *wobbly old-timers*. He turned around, beaming.

'That's my son!' he said happily.

*

Over at Fly Cutz, Big Tyrone clicked off his clippers, then put one hand on his waist and the other one up high in the air. He closed his eyes and starting gyrating his middle.

'I love this song!' he said.

'Yeah, we can tell!' said one of the customers.

Big Tyrone kissed his teeth, laughed, then carried on winding his waist. Clipper FM was his new favourite radio station, by far.

'Next!' he shouted.

*

'OK, OK, *OK*,' said Kofi energetically, leaning further towards the mic. 'You're locked into the sounds of the one and only *Clipper FM*, live and loud, from the top of the block, straight into your ears! This is the one and only MC Coinboy, and that was a little bit of Calippo—'

'*Calypso*,' whispered Kelvin.

'I mean, calyp-*so*,' Kofi corrected himself, 'for a sunny Saturday afternoon . . .'

He beckoned over to Kelvin and Leroy, pointing at an unoccupied microphone stand.

'Now get ready to up the tempo with some fresh new bars from *Kels the Reloader* and *Young L*! You guys ready?'

'Of course!' yelled Leroy.

'Yep!' said Kelvin.

'T – drop the beat!' grinned Kofi.

Acknowledgements

First of all, thanks to everyone at Faber who helped bring this book to life. Huge thanks to Leah Thaxton, Bethany Carter, Natasha Brown and the whole Faber Children's team. A special thanks to Stephanie King for all those tweaks and edits that helped get the story into such great shape. Appreciated!

As always, a massive thank you to my agent extraordinaire, Sarah Such of the Sarah Such Literary Agency, for all the support, wisdom and guidance. I'm proud to work with you.

My family! Sophie, our two boys, Finlay and Blake, my mother, Mary, and two big sisters, Phyllis and Marcia. I've been inspired and supported by all of you in so many different ways. Big thanks also to all my cousins and friends who I grew up with. Kofi's world is the same one we all lived in back in the 1990s. Special times.

And finally, thank YOU for jumping in and spending time with Kofi, his friends and family and me. It means everything to have the support of readers of all ages and if you've made it this far, I hope you've enjoyed all the adventures as much as I have.

Don't miss Kofi's first adventure!

'A cracking book.'
Frank Cottrell-Boyce

KOFI and the RAP BATTLE SUMMER

JEFFREY BOAKYE

Kofi had an idea . . . one big lightning bolt of an idea that hit him like electricity. And all it needed was Kelvin's incredible memory for words.

Kofi is used to stuff going wrong, he's usually in detention or about to be. But when he finds out his best friend Kelvin has a photographic memory, he comes up with a **genius money-making scheme**. The whole school is obsessed with **music**, but no one can ever make out the words, so the boys hit the jackpot selling a new fanzine full of song lyrics: **PAPER JAM**. It's not long before one of the teacher's tells Kofi: 'You could be a real leader at this school, you know that?' and . . . suddenly it's turning out to be **the best summer *ever*!**

Take a walk through musical history...

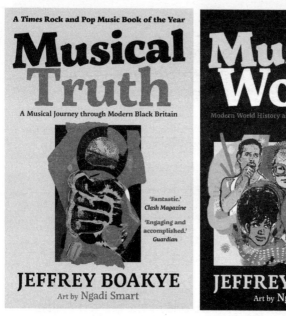
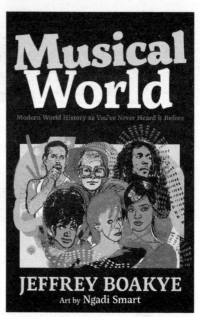